"I can't go through with this," Jackson said.

"Dressing up as a woman is the only way you're going to get close to Purity. If you want to win your bet," Darla said. "Don't worry. I'll show you how to walk and talk. Now, if you'll just slip into this bra…"

It was only a bra. Shoot, Jackson had seen enough of them in his time. Feeling like a complete idiot, he thrust his strong forearms through the arm loops, then shrugged them onto his rounded, powerful shoulders.

The foam-filled D cups were huge. Darla reached around and hooked the strap.

Jackson wasn't proud of it, but his heart suddenly thudded in panic. It seemed as if his fate had been sealed somehow—as if there was no turning back now. Even worse, he realized the cups were lopsided. It looked as if a strong wind had just come along and knocked the breasts galley-west.

With a grimace, Jackson grabbed each of the cushioned cups. Darn. They were harder to wrestle than a calf from a mama cow. He hadn't had this much trouble with a bra since he was in high school—and the wearer was a girl. Lordy, he'd never hear the end of it if the guys found out about this.

"This thing pinches," he complained.

"Welcome to womanhood, Jackson!" Darla exclaimed perkily. "Wait until you try panty hose!"

Dear Reader,

The comic antics continue with two very different but equally wonderful romantic comedies!

Longtime reader favorite Cathie Linz has joined the LOVE & LAUGHTER lineup with a very special trilogy called MARRIAGE MAKERS. Susan Elizabeth Phillips says, "Cathie Linz's fun and lively romances are guaranteed to win readers' hearts! A shining star of the romance genre." Jennifer Greene adds, "Every book has sparkle and wit; Cathie is truly a unique voice in the genre." Cathie is also the winner of the *Romantic Times* Storyteller of the Year Award, as well as being nominated for Career Achievement in Love and Laughter. Her trilogy about the Knight triplets includes lots of emotion, comedy and the antics of some well-intentioned but bumbling fairy godmothers.

Jule McBride spins a fabulous tale in *How the West Was Wed,* part of our Western mini marathon. A three-time Reviewer's Choice nominee for "Best American Romance," Jule McBride has also been nominated for two lifetime achievement awards in the category of "Love and Laughter." When Jule, a native of West Virginia, was little she kept her books inside her grandmother Helen's carved oak cabinet, to which only she had the key. Only later did Jule realize that the characters she loved weren't real and that someone called a "writer" conjured them. That's when she knew one day she'd be a writer. And Jule has created very memorable and hilarious characters in this story of a cross-dressing cowboy! (Really, he's the hero. It's fun— think Tom Hanks and Robin Williams.)

Enjoy the love and laughter,

Malle Vallik

Malle Vallik
Associate Senior Editor

HOW THE WEST WAS WED
Jule McBride

Harlequin Books

TORONTO • NEW YORK • LONDON
AMSTERDAM • PARIS • SYDNEY • HAMBURG
STOCKHOLM • ATHENS • TOKYO • MILAN
MADRID • WARSAW • BUDAPEST • AUCKLAND

ISBN 0-373-44046-4

HOW THE WEST WAS WED

Copyright © 1998 by Julianne Randolph Moore

A funny thing happened...

"Can I write about a cross-dressing cowboy?" I asked my LOVE & LAUGHTER editor. A long silence ensued. "Well," she said, "that might be good—as a second book." I said fine and quickly wrote a first book (LOVE & LAUGHTER #23), *Who's Been Sleeping in My Bed?* Then I called back and said, "Now can we do the cross-dressing cowboy?"

The answer was yes. And I'm so glad! I had great fun writing *How the West Was Wed.* It's about Jackson West, a hard-drinking, hard-loving Montana cowboy who—in order to rope and bed a woman and win a saloon wager— has absolutely no other option but to don a dress and work as her housekeeper. Jackson, of course, is the last man you'd expect to be caught with his—ahem—pants down. He's a sexy rancher who, although he's tough on the exterior, turns out to have a heart of gold.

I hope you get a chuckle watching macho Jackson West get in touch with his more female, sensitive side!

Jule McBride

Don't miss Jule McBride's summer titles, kicking off with Bridal Showers, *an anthology, in April, followed by two new* BIG APPLE BABIES *miniseries titles at American Romance:* Diagnosis: Daddy *in May and* A.K.A.: Marriage *in July.*

Books by Jule McBride

HARLEQUIN LOVE & LAUGHTER
23—WHO'S BEEN SLEEPING IN MY BED?

HARLEQUIN AMERICAN ROMANCE
658—COLE IN MY STOCKING
693—MISSION: MOTHERHOOD
699—VERDICT: PARENTHOOD

Don't miss any of our special offers. Write to us at the following address for information on our newest releases.

Harlequin Reader Service
U.S.: 3010 Walden Ave., P.O. Box 1325, Buffalo, NY 14269
Canadian: P.O. Box 609, Fort Erie, Ont. L2A 5X3

For J. F. Jacobson—
the coolest cowboy in L.A.

1

"I SWEAR—" Jackson West's laconic drawl was directed at no one in particular "—if I hear one more word about that thirty-pound bull trout Logan Hatcher pulled out of the river, I'm headin' right back to the ranch."

Jackson was just as tired of talking about knapweed, last summer's drought and the worst predator to ever threaten the endangered wildlife of Montana, which meant Californians. In fact, Jackson had already heard every conversation taking place inside Dusty's Moose Head Saloon at least a thousand times before. What he needed was some excitement. A new challenge. Not to mention a warm, willing woman.

Jackson stared hopefully down Dusty's bar, but all he saw was a long line of cowboys in Wrangler jeans, plaid shirts, boots and Western-style hats. All were standing; an unseasonable snow up on Miracle Mountain had forced an early autumn roundup, so even men born to the saddle were too sore to sit, including Jackson. The good news was that made women easier to spot, since they were the only folks sitting down on the bar stools. The bad news was that all eleven women in Dusty's were either happily married or directly related to Jackson.

On Jackson's right, his sister, Darla, had spread her fanzines on the bar. On his left, his brother, Austin, twined fingers with his wife, Crystal, who was six months pregnant with the baby that would make Jackson an uncle six times over. The rest of Jackson's siblings—there were seven Wests altogether—milled with their spouses around Dusty's, which was more a friendly pub than a hard-drinking establishment. Everybody looked so cozy. Whereas Jackson—eldest of the West clan and head of the Bar Triple Cross since their daddy's death—was about to face his thirty-third cold Montana winter alone. Which was the real reason Jackson was in such a bad mood.

He'd thought his problems were solved when he'd met a cute therapist in the nearby town of Silver Spoon. Trouble was, she'd kept trying to analyze him. On their first date, she'd announced he was the strong, silent cowboy type—and it wasn't a compliment. Then, on the second date, she'd shown him a psychology textbook, in which it said that every man—Jackson included—possessed something called a Freudian Oedipal complex. That meant, whether Jackson realized it or not, he was cursed by a secret, subconscious desire to sleep with his own mother. It was, hands down, the most insane thing Jackson had ever heard.

Last night had been the icing on the cake. The therapist had asked him to drive over so they could "have a little chat." When she'd served herbal tea in a cup so dainty his calloused hand wrapped around it twice, Jackson should have guessed he was in a heap of trouble. And sure enough, after much throat clearing, she'd asked him to go to couples' counseling.

Maybe he was wrong. But in the world according to Jackson, three dinner dates weren't enough for any woman—even a trained therapist—to decide he lacked a sensitive side. So he'd nipped the romance in the bud—and broke up. Still, he'd lain awake all last night, staring at the ceiling and worrying. At this rate, he'd never get hitched.

"Darla—" Jackson turned to his little sister "—do I lack a sensitive side?"

Darla stared up from her fanzines. His sister had his same golden hair and cornflower blue eyes. "You?" Darla said. "A sensitive side?" And then she burst out laughing.

"Thanks for the vote of confidence, Darla."

Jackson turned back to the bar, his gaze taking in the moose head mounted over the bar mirror. An Easter bonnet was nestled between the antlers which, in turn, were still strung with last year's Christmas lights. With true cowboy machismo, Dusty always swore he'd "hunted down that moose and killed it like a man." But everybody knew the poor animal had really died of old age in the saloon owner's backyard. Dusty couldn't kill anything if his life depended on it.

Dusty, Jackson thought enviously, had a sensitive side.

Scrutinizing himself in the bar mirror, Jackson decided he didn't *look* insensitive. He had hay-colored hair, a lick of which fell from beneath his tan Stetson and curled on his forehead, and squinty blue eyes women described as dreamy. His body was typical of most cowboys, with big, bronzed callused hands, a strong torso, a slim bony behind and rangy, muscular bowed legs. Oh, he was a little unpolished—used to roughhousing, and some hard drinking and betting on occasion, especially with his best buddy and favorite competitor, Logan Hatcher. But then, Jackson was a healthy thirty-three-year-old rancher; working hard and playing hard came with the territory.

He must have looked worried, because his sister finally sighed. "Sorry, Jackson. But you've played footsies with every available woman between here and Bozeman.''

Because Bozeman was hundreds of miles due south, Jackson started to protest, but then he decided maybe Darla had a point. ''Why, sure,'' he drawled. ''But that's because I *like* women. Doesn't that make me sensitive?''

Darla rolled her eyes heavenward. After a moment, she smiled indulgently. ''Lighten up. No matter what your girlfriends say, I'll always love you, Jackson. Besides, big brother, you're so cute you don't really need to be sensitive.''

But obviously he did. At least if he wanted a wife. Shrugging off his women troubles, Jackson zeroed in on the conversations circling around the bar. Thankfully, Logan had quit bragging about his oversize trout. Now the topic was Californians again.

''Most celebrities buy down around Bozeman or Livingston, not here,'' Austin was saying. ''And I, for one, think Montana would be a better place if they'd all hop on their horses and ride off into the sunset. Just like in the movies, which is where they belong.''

''But why would she come now, right before winter?'' Crystal asked. ''Celebrities always clear out by September.''

She? Jackson's ears perked up. ''She who?''

''Purity,'' said Austin.

Jackson had never heard of her. ''Who?''

''Ask Darla,'' teased Logan from the other end of the bar. ''She's best friends with everybody in New York and Hollywood.''

That drew a few chuckles, since Darla read fanzines religiously and habitually talked about celebrities as if they were her next of kin. Darla riffled through some pages, then slid a picture toward Jackson. She tapped the page with a perfectly manicured nail. "That's Purity."

Pure wasn't how Jackson would have described her. She was in her twenties, with wavy platinum-blond, jaw-length hair. A sexy mole was beside her pouty mouth, and she had a voluptuous body—full breasts and hips. In the picture, she was strutting across a stage, dressed for sin in short cutoffs and a black leather lace-up corset with bra cups spangled in silver studs. Absently, Jackson's hand rose to his chest, and he rubbed his palm on his plaid flannel shirt, over his heart. Loosing his most soulful wolf whistle, he softly drawled, "Now *there's* a warm, willing woman."

"Oh, Jackson," Darla said in censure. "I feel sorry for her. She just got dumped!"

Even though Purity was a celebrity—and nothing more to him than a picture in a fanzine—Jackson's chest squeezed tight. Was this sinful-looking blond woman really available? "I've never heard of her," Jackson murmured, still staring wistfully at the picture.

"She sings heavy metal music," Darla informed him.

Jackson shrugged. He kept the radio in his pickup tuned to country-western. "What's her last name?"

"She only has one name," Darla continued conversationally. "You know, like Cher or Madonna. But if she doesn't sign her new contract, she won't have a name at all. She'll be a has-been."

Austin shook his head in mock horror. "Imagine. Becoming a has-been at that age!"

"Austin, you were a has-been before you were born," Jackson returned, winking at his sister-in-law, who'd learned to take the ribbing between the West men in stride.

"At least I've got a woman to keep me warm this

winter...." Austin's fingers tightened through those of his pregnant wife. "Which is more than I can say for you, Jackson."

Tipping back his Stetson, Jackson chuckled. "Oh, c'mon, Austin. After Darla and Crystal dressed you up like a woman for last year's annual Halloween dance, you *had* to marry Crystal just to save your masculine pride."

Logan hooted from the other end of the bar. "Austin sure did have sexy legs, though. Didn't he, Jackson?"

"Cleavage, too," agreed Jackson.

"I did a good job on that costume," Darla said defensively.

"You did." Jackson grinned at the memory of his little brother, decked out in a blue sequined gown and high heels. If Jackson hadn't known better, he would have asked his own brother to dance.

Logan said, "He looked enough like a bona fide woman to scare the tar out of me."

"It was Halloween," Darla shot back, "He was supposed to be scary."

Logan winked. "Hey, Jackson, Halloween's only weeks away. Maybe this year you'll be Darla's next victim."

Darla actually looked hopeful.

Jackson frowned down at his kid sister. Darla's dream was to get a job in Hollywood as a makeup artist. For now, she owned a hair salon, which had also—because of the gossip that ran rampant inside—become a job placement agency. The sign in the salon window said Hair, Makeovers And Employment Networking. "You'll never get me in a dress, Darla," Jackson assured her.

From the other end of the bar, Logan suddenly whistled. "Not the McGregor place!"

"Wait a minute," Austin said. "Did Purity buy the McGregor place?"

Darla nodded.

"The McGregor place?" Crystal echoed in horror.

Jackson kept his mouth shut. Nobody knew that he, not a McGregor relative back east, had owned the old McGregor property.

"I've got a Californian living next to me?" Logan roared, spitting out the word *Californian* as if it were the vilest curse.

"I think she's really from New York," Darla said helpfully.

Jackson bit back a smile. "See, Logan," he drawled, "if you'd sold me that strip of land I've been trying to buy from you for the last fifteen years, then it would be me, not you, who was sharing a property line with a Californian."

Logan scowled. "If I have to live next to ten Californians, you're not getting that property, Jackson."

Jackson merely shrugged. Somehow he'd figure out a scheme to get that land. He'd hoped selling the adjacent lot to a Californian would force Logan to sell, but now he guessed not.

Austin was squinting. "And Purity paid how much?"

"She told me a half million dollars," said Darla.

Crystal gasped. "She paid that much? And you actually *talked* to Purity, Darla? *The* Purity?"

Darla hemmed and hawed, saying she had a responsibility to protect Purity's privacy, but then she admitted, "Purity contacted me after she saw the employment networking sign in my salon window as she drove into town. She needs a housekeeper. She's madder than a hornet that she accidentally paid so much money for that cow camp shack."

Jackson winced. Maybe his description of the property in the *Los Angeles Times* ad had stretched the truth, but he'd never expected some high-toned agent to call and offer such an outrageous sum, sight unseen. Of course Jackson had taken the money. After all, he was a businessman, in charge of the largest ranch in this part of Montana. He'd had no idea who the real buyer was—until now. He feigned only casual interest. "Purity's looking for a *housekeeper?*"

"That shack needs a wrecking crew!" Logan exploded. "Nobody could *live* there!"

Darla shook her head, clearly scandalized. "It doesn't even have an indoor toilet, just a bathtub, and there's only a woodstove for heat! When I talked to her, she was really mad. I mean, *screaming* mad. She said she was besieged by reporters and that she didn't want to see anybody—especially not any men. She just wants one person to come. A lady, who can straighten up the place for her and run errands."

"And so you're really supposed to find her a housekeeper?" Crystal asked.

Darla nodded. "I said I would."

"You know," Crystal continued in a near non sequitur, "when our church group visited that poor little girl who's in the hospital down in Silver Spoon, she mentioned that Purity was her favorite singer."

Jackson nearly groaned out loud. The meandering conversations in Dusty's always came full circle, so he should have known this subject would resurface. Last week, a couple from Wyoming had wrecked their car in front of Dusty's, and their twelve-year-old daughter was still in the hospital in the adjacent town. Jackson felt so bad about the injured little girl that he could barely stand to hear about it.

"Hey," Austin said now, "I wager Jackson could

figure out how to get Purity's autograph for that poor little girl.''

Crystal's eyes went soft. ''Oh, I bet he could! You can figure out how to do anything, can't you, Jackson?''

Darla shook her head. ''Since she got dumped, Purity *really* doesn't want men anywhere near her.''

In spite of Darla's warning, one thing led to another—until Austin was saying, ''Now, Jackson, if you get Purity's autograph for that little girl, then me and the hands promise we'll vaccinate all the cattle without your help this year.''

Jackson had to admit that sounded good.

''And you get me a corset similar to that—'' Dusty leaned over Darla and pointed at Purity's leather, silver-studded top in the magazine picture ''—and I'll buy your drinks for a month.''

Jackson couldn't help but chuckle. ''I don't mean to pry, Dusty,'' he drawled, ''but why would you want a corset?''

Dusty pointed his thumb toward the moose head above the bar. ''It'll keep her from catching cold this winter.''

Jackson guffawed, imagining the moose clad in the Easter bonnet, Christmas lights and Purity's corset.

''I'll go everybody one better,'' Logan called out.

Darla groaned. ''I knew this was coming.''

Logan chuckled. ''First, Jackson gets the autograph, then he gets the corset. And then, if he *sleeps* with Purity—'' Logan absently touched the brim of his Stetson and flashed a wide grin around the saloon ''—I'll give him that strip of land he's been trying to buy from me for the last fifteen years.''

Jackson didn't know why, but he and his best buddy had been going head to head since they'd first locked horns in grade school. Jackson said, "What proof would you need?"

Logan shrugged. "Just your word."

Jackson nodded. He'd never lied to win a bet. "You'll give me the deed to that land if I sleep with her?"

"Have sex," Logan clarified. "And with one stipulation. To get to the McGregor place, you can't hop my electric fence or go through the Simpsons' property. To meet her, you have to go right in through her front gate."

That didn't sound too difficult until Darla spoke up. "Too bad, Jackson. The McGregor place is locked up tighter than a drum. There's news media camped out in front and the sheriff from Silver Spoon is making sure no one gets past except the housekeepers I'm setting up for Purity to interview."

"Ha," said Logan, looking satisfied. "You'd have to get through all those people just to say hello to the woman, Jackson. And Purity won't see any men. Looks like you've lost to me again, buddy."

But Jackson was determined to get his hands on the land Logan was offering. "Want to bet?"

Logan grinned. "Looks like we just did, partner."

Jackson realized Darla was gaping at him. "Did I do something wrong, Darla?"

"Why, heavens no, Jackson. You just made a bet that involves having sex with a woman you've never even met." Darla sighed wearily and turned her fanzine page. "Pray tell," she continued, "is this your sensitive side in action again?"

"This is a bad idea," Jackson drawled, even as he unbuttoned his plaid flannel shirt and shrugged out of it.

"Quit fidgeting!" Darla exclaimed. "And quit complaining. When Howard Stern promoted his book, he wore a gold sequined dress on the David Letterman show. Even one of the mayors of New York, Rudolph Giuliani, dressed in a gown for a fundraiser. Robin Williams did it in the movie *Mrs. Doubtfire*, and Dustin Hoffman was a woman in *Tootsie*—"

"Dustin Hoffman doesn't drink in Dusty's," Jackson reminded her, feeling suddenly testy.

Not that Darla noticed. "And just think—" her clipped rational tone was becoming annoying "—a century ago, women weren't even allowed to wear pants. And now they can wear almost anything—suits and ties, boxer shorts and combat boots."

"Great," said Jackson dryly. He'd rather see a woman in a short skirt and high heels any day.

"It *is* great."

"And this is *really* a bad idea." Jackson winced as his sister tweezed yet another recalcitrant hair from his upper lip.

"Without my written recommendation and unless you're dressed for the housekeeper's job," Darla warned, "you'll never get past the security at Purity's front gate."

"Believe me," Jackson said through clenched teeth, "I've already considered every possible option. And anyway, I thought you were totally against this bet I made with Logan."

"Oh, I think you're both totally juvenile."

"So why are you helping me?"

Darla steadied herself against his bare shoulder, then dabbed foundation on his forehead with a sponge. "First, because I now have the toughest cowboy in Northern Montana at my mercy. Second, because turning you into a woman is a showcase for my talents. And third, because it's my civic duty.''

"What is?"

"Making sure my big brother doesn't take advantage of women. Purity just got dumped by one jerk." Darla suddenly grinned, looking mighty pleased with herself. "I figure you can't seduce her if you have to wear a dress."

"You've got a point there," Jackson murmured, still wondering how he was going to accomplish the last part of his three-tier mission—sleeping with Purity so he could get his hands on Logan's land.

"Besides," Darla continued, "dressed this way, I do think you might get Purity's autograph for that little girl who's in the hospital. And I think that's sweet." Darla stepped back and scrutinized Jackson, tilting her head this way and that. "You might even get one of her corsets."

He'd get the land from Logan, too. It was all that kept the Wests' ranch, the Bar Triple Cross, from having a southern road access. Jackson glanced around grimly. So far, the closest he'd gotten to Purity was Wyatt Simpson's rustic cabin next door. It smelled of booze and stale tobacco, and Wyatt was passed out in the other room.

Catching Jackson's gaze, Darla shook her head. "You're sure Wyatt won't mind us being here?"

"Positive."

Darla began tweezing Jackson's lip again. "What a waste of a good man."

Jackson nodded. He'd felt so sorry for Wyatt, who's drinking had worsened after his parents died, that when Wyatt could no longer make payments on this property, Jackson had anonymously bought it. That way, the bank wouldn't foreclose and turn the young man out onto the street. When Wyatt was sober enough, Jackson gave him work on the ranch. Sometimes he'd also drop by with cash or groceries, hoping to talk Wyatt, who was Darla's age, into sobering up. Wyatt had been the water boy for Jackson's high school football team, and Jackson could still remember his bright-eyed eagerness, his dark-eyed good looks. Now, Wyatt's once sparkling eyes were bloodshot, his glossy black hair was unkempt, as were his scraggly black beard and mustache.

Well, for the moment, Jackson's efforts to help Wyatt amounted to one thing—he could use this cabin. If Wyatt woke up and realized what Jackson was doing, he'd help keep it hush-hush. Jackson couldn't have changed clothes at the ranch, not with the cowhands around. And if the guys in Dusty's ever got wind of—

"I can't go through with this," Jackson suddenly said.

"It's the only way," Darla said. "Don't worry. I'll show you how to walk and talk. And I promise I won't tell a soul. Now, if you'll just slip on this bra…"

She held the thing up by the shoulder loops. "Darla…"

"Now, c'mon," she coaxed. "I know it would take a lot more than white lace to unman a rough wrangler like you.…"

Well, Darla was right. It was only a bra. Shoot, Jackson had seen enough of them in his time. Still, he felt as if he was about to mount a horse from a hayloft. *Just don't look down, buddy.* Feeling like a complete idiot, he thrust his strong bronzed corded forearms through the arm loops, then shrugged them onto his rounded, powerful shoulders.

"Thatta boy," crooned Darla, patting his back.

It turned out to be the same bra Austin had worn

last Halloween. The foam-filled D cups were huge. Darla reached around and hooked the strap.

Jackson wasn't proud of it, but his heart suddenly thudded in panic. It seemed as if his fate had been sealed somehow—as if there was no turning back now. Even worse, he realized the cups were lopsided. It looked as if a strong wind had just come along and knocked the breasts galley-west.

With a grimace, Jackson grabbed each of the cushioned cups. Darn. They were harder to wrestle than a calf from a mama cow. He hadn't had this much trouble with a bra since he was in high school—and the wearer was a girl. *I can't believe I'm doing this. Where's my cowboy pride?* Lordy, he'd never hear the end of this if the guys in Dusty's found out. Or his ranch hands. Not to mention the therapist he'd dated down in Silver Spoon. In her book, dressing as a woman was probably even worse than having a Freudian Oedipal complex. Jackson would probably wind up committed to a padded cell....

He grunted testily. "This thing pinches."

"Welcome to womanhood, Jackson!" Darla exclaimed perkily. "Wait until you try panty hose!"

He shot her a quelling glance. "I think you're actually enjoying yourself."

Darla grinned. "Immensely." She crossed the room and began riffling through Wyatt's mother's wardrobe. "Mrs. Simpson's been gone for years," she murmured conversationally. "I can't believe Wyatt never even cleaned out her closet."

Darla's glance darted back and forth between Jackson and the row of shapeless cotton jumpers that had been Mrs. Simpson's trademark, finally lifting out one printed with large, splotchy red and orange flowers. "Here," she said, returning from the closet. "First, slip on this turtleneck, then the jumper. You can wear these blue-framed glasses—the lenses don't seem very strong—and one of Mrs. Simpson's old wigs, as well as carry this red pocketbook.... Hmm. Now I want you to kick off your boots, shuck your jeans and put on these opaque stockings. They're so thick that no one will notice those hairy legs of yours." Darla made another trip to the closet. "And these walking boots look big enough...."

"If anybody finds out about this—" Jackson steadfastly tried to ignore the cushioned falsies brushing his arms as he pulled on the stockings "—I'll have to move to Wyoming."

"Believe me, even Mom wouldn't recognize you now," Darla said when they were done. She stood back and sighed with satisfaction. "Perfect! Well, aren't you even going to look?"

Darla's grin told Jackson he wasn't going to like what he saw. Slowly he turned toward the mirror. His jaw went slack. "Darla," he growled threateningly.

She raised her eyebrows innocently. "Hmm?"

He shot her a long, malevolent look.

When she saw his venomous expression, Darla's shoulders started shaking with barely suppressed laughter. "Now, Jackson," she crooned, "we can't all be fairy princesses!"

Feeling faintly murderous, he stared into the mirror again.

He *did* look like a woman. In fact, it was an amazing—if very unsettling—transformation.

Trouble was, Jackson looked like the late Mrs. Simpson. And that meant he wasn't exactly the best-looking female around. A sturdy mountaineer, Mrs. Simpson had been even larger boned than Jackson. She'd possessed some facial hair and had worn gray wigs to hide her thinning scalp. At least that's how Jackson remembered her. The truth was, Mrs. Simpson—who was rumored to have drunk as much as her son—hadn't been seen in Miracle Mountain for years, and most people assumed she'd died.

"Well, aren't you going to say something, Jackson?"

"No."

He simply couldn't believe this. His well-hewn body looked as shapeless as a potato sack in the gaudy jumper. The wild print of the fabric drew the eye away from his face, which he guessed was good, since it further disguised him, but he looked closer to sixty years old than thirty-three. While the turtleneck hid his Adam's apple and softened the line of his jaw, the blue glasses added homeliness, as did the gray wig hair that scraggled almost to his shoulders, and the thick black leggings that were bagging at his knees. Jackson finally exploded, "This looks awful! Isn't there a dress in that closet without flowers, Darla?"

With a sudden hoot, Darla crumpled against the wall, laughing so hard that she doubled over. After a long moment, she got her shoulder-shaking giggles under control. Cocking her head, she cupped a hand around her ear. "Hark, is this vanity I hear? Why, Jackson, maybe this will put you in touch with your more female, sensitive side, after all." Slapping her thigh, Darla started giggling uncontrollably again, this time until tears of merriment clung to her eyelashes. Finally she managed to say, "Sorry. All the solid-colored jumpers need ironing."

Jackson felt defeated. "I don't know how to iron."

"Then I guess you're wearing flowers." Darla chortled.

His angry expression merely sent Darla into another gale of giggles.

Go ahead and get it out of your system, Darla. It would take a lot more than laughter to unman him. Jackson grabbed a comb and started yanking it through the scraggly strands of the gray wig. "Well," he muttered, "no celebrity would ever hire somebody who looks like this. So at least I know I'm in no danger of actually getting that housekeeper's job."

The words sent Darla into yet another bout of hysterical laughter. "Only your—your—"

"Only my what?" he ground out.

"Only your hairdresser knows for sure," she gasped.

Something in her tone should have given Jackson pause. But he was too busy squaring his shoulders. Putting his hands on his hips, he turned slowly from side to side, finally deciding the breasts looked real enough.

"Ah," Darla said with a sigh, still shaky from all her laughter at his expense. "It's like beauty and the beast."

Jackson's tone was grim. "I take it I'm the beast?"

"Oh, Jackson," she purred, "you're so sensitive *and* smart."

Shooting Darla a last lethal stare, Jackson turned to the mirror again. A hulking, middle-aged mountaineer woman with gray hair, blue-framed glasses, a wildly printed dress and red pocketbook stared back. Fortunately, Jackson thought, every dark cloud had a silver lining.

He was about to meet—and sleep with—the juiciest blond bombshell on the planet.

2

CLUTCHING THE SHORT STRAPS of the old-fashioned red pocketbook, Jackson stared at Purity through the screen door of her shack. He was doing his level best to hold down the hem of the red-and-orange floral-print jumper, which was blowing wildly in the autumn wind.

"Get out of here!" Purity shrieked.

Her fingernails, long silver-painted talons, were tightly wrapped around a portable phone receiver. As she paced across the leaf-strewn floor, the jingle of her myriad necklaces was punctuated by the metal taps of knee-high, pink patent-leather combat boots. Pink boxer shorts peeked from beneath her denim cutoffs, and she wore a fluffy, pink wool sweater open over a black leather corset. So many pink earrings studded her ear rims that Jackson couldn't count them all; her lipstick was some shade that resembled black more than plum; and even though the room was illuminated only by a bald overhead bulb, her eyes remained hidden by black, wraparound sunglasses. Jackson had no idea what he thought about her outfit—except that it was very pink and color coordinated.

"Oh, no!" she shrieked. "Get *out!*"

Jackson still couldn't move.

Her voice was made to project in a stadium, not a tumbledown three-room shack; it vibrated right through him. He hazarded a quick glance through the screen at the room's flimsy walls, half expecting them to shudder and crumble. Beneath her ample breasts, he decided, the woman must have lungs the size of Texas. But how could a voice that loud be so soft? The decibel level aside, it was like honey and molasses, and it reminded him of rich, warm things such as the velvety winter coats on wild horses.

"Get out of here already!"

No doubt it was his outfit. Shoot, *he* wouldn't hire someone who looked like an aging female version of the Incredible Hulk. Apparently, Purity wasn't even going to let him in for the interview. Relief swept through him. As much as he wanted to win the bet with Logan, Jackson had certainly been dreading this. Still clutching both the pocketbook and the jumper hem, he turned to go.

"Not you!" With a quick, stabbing motion of a metallic fingernail, Purity gestured toward a couch covered with a clean bedsheet.

Jackson wavered.

Shoving the phone between her jaw and ear, Purity threw up her hands and glared at Jackson through the screen. "Get out of here," she snapped. "It's just an expression. It doesn't mean for you to leave. It means…" She heaved a loud sigh as if he was the most impossible domestic worker on the planet. "Oh, I don't know what it means! Just come in and sit down!"

Jackson was so stunned, he still couldn't move. Darla had compared him to the fairy-tale Beast. But Purity was no doe-eyed Beauty; she was more like the hellcat in *The Taming of the Shrew*. No woman had ever raised her voice to him this way. In his wildest nightmares, he couldn't imagine sleeping with this she-devil. But thinking of Logan's land, he forced himself to head inside the cabin. As he seated himself on the couch, a cloud of dust puffed around him, and he loosed a very male-sounding sneeze.

Not that Purity noticed, or much less said, "God bless you." She was already screaming into the phone again, stalking between the living room's two windows. Yanking back a tattered, yellowed curtain, she scowled toward the media. "I'm not signing that contract," she snarled into the phone. "Why? Because I'm about to turn thirty years old, that's why! And when I'm fifty, I hardly envision myself singing with Abel Rage and a heavy metal band called the Trash Cans!"

For long moments, Purity merely paced, her head bobbing up and down, her pink combat boots clomping. Then she yelled, "What's wrong with suburbia? I bet I would have been *happy* in suburbia. Just give me two-point-five kids—" She paused in midsentence, looking stunned. "Oh, the statistic's down to one-point-four?" Her voice had dropped to a reasonable level, but now it spiked again. "Well, throw in a dog and a station wagon! They should be worth a point!"

Jackson winced at the tirade. No wonder she had boyfriend problems. Should he risk an escape? Unable to decide, he glanced around the dingy room, which opened onto a bedroom and kitchen. His eyes slunk toward the later, when he remembered there was a back door.

Well, no matter how bad an impression she was making, Jackson couldn't let her stay in this ramshackle dive. The Christian thing would be for him to apologize and then give her money back. Forget the bet, he decided. When she got off the phone, he'd convince her to return to California. Later he'd contact the woman who'd handled the deal, and he'd repurchase the land.

He just hoped Purity didn't realize he was a man

when she heard his voice. Deciding not to entertain the possibility, he continued looking around. He hadn't checked on this place for a while. Nature had been encroaching, and leaves and twigs littered the scarred wood floor. To Jackson's right was a wood-burning stove that probably hadn't been used for years. Behind him, silver-backed insulation peeked from between beams in an exposed section of the wall. Various items leaned in a corner, among them a broom and an old rifle he couldn't believe the local kids hadn't taken. They'd been inside, judging from the empty soda cans and stubs of burned-down candles.

Purity's belongings stood out like sore thumbs—two spiffy black carry-ons next to the door, and a shiny, white Land Rover off-road vehicle that was parked in the weeds outside, next to a stack of car tires and a junked refrigerator. Jackson's eyes strayed to the bald lightbulb in the ceiling. At least she'd had the electricity turned on.

As guilty as he felt, he wished she'd quit ignoring him. If he was dressed as a man, would she get off the phone? Jackson made a vow to be more attentive in the future to all women in service occupations. If he happened to be on the phone when one arrived at the ranch office for a job interview, he'd hang up immediately.

Shoot, Jackson, just be grateful she's not scrutinizing your outfit. Realizing his knees had naturally drifted apart for the umpteenth time, he sighed miserably. As he crossed his ankles in what he hoped was a ladylike fashion, Mrs. Simpson's mountaineer boots squeezed his toes.

Jackson shook his head. He'd spent hours in the saddle, slept in unheated cow camp shacks up in the mountains during roundups, and pitched hay until he thought his back would break. But in all his born days, he'd never been this uncomfortable. The bra was torturously tight, and the leggings—so baggy at the knees—pinched at the waist and were darn near cutting off his breath. When he'd complained, Darla had merely offered him a garter belt as an alternative to panty hose. He'd said no, of course. Hell, a man had to draw the line somewhere.

Jackson made another vow. From now on, he'd make sure his dates really wanted to go places where they had to wear dresses, uncomfortable bras and panty hose.

At least Purity had turned out to be physically gorgeous—a real vision with pale, poreless skin and hair that looked as soft as finely spun silk. She had well-toned arms and legs, and she moved quickly and gracefully, radiating raw energy. Jackson could have watched her for hours, mesmerized.

At least until she opened her mouth.

"What do I look like?" she shrieked now. "Chopped liver?" She paced, nodded, jingled and clanked some more. Then she bellowed, "I am *not* leaving here!"

But she had to.

As if to prove the point, a field mouse suddenly darted across the floor. No doubt, if Purity noticed the mouse, she'd hightail it for her Land Rover. Mustering the falsetto voice he'd practiced with Darla, Jackson waved his arms wildly in the air and called out, "Oh, dear! Oh, dear! A mouse! A mouse!"

Purity whirled around. Sensing her attention, the terrified mouse paused, quivering against a baseboard. Purity stalked toward it, then she jumped up and down in her pink combat boots. The mouse fled, and Purity's sunglass-covered eyes followed until it vanished through a hole in the floorboards.

Slowly turning toward Jackson, Purity shook her head in total disgust. "For God's sake, lady," she said, "it's just a mouse." And then she turned her back and started pacing and screaming into the phone again.

As if he didn't know it was just a mouse, Jackson thought disgustedly. He crossed his arms over his chest, completely forgetting about his triple-D chest. Grimacing, he lowered his forearms and settled them uncomfortably across his taut belly. Glancing down, he winced again at the bright fabric that covered his lap.

"You don't think I should stay here?" Purity burst out now. "You're the one who paid so much of my hard-earned money for this place!" Her voice rose to a fever pitch. "And when I get my hands on that man Jackson West, he won't know what hit him!"

Great. She knows I'm the previous owner of the property. Jackson fought the urge to muster his falsetto and put in a good word for Jackson West. But the less he talked, the better. Already, he'd had a bout with terror when he'd conversed with the sheriff. True to the stipulation of the bet, Jackson had entered the property through Purity's front gate. Fortunately, he'd never met the sheriff from Silver Spoon. Still, the middle-aged man had thoroughly questioned him while the citified news people back at the roadblock had stared on curiously.

Jackson had almost reached Purity's door when he'd heard a low, loud wolf whistle. For all he knew, the sheriff had been the culprit. He hadn't turned around, of course. Even now, it made Jackson feel furious. He'd felt so…on display. Like an object. Hell, he fumed now, at least *he* had the decency to only whistle at young, pretty women.

Lordy, he really had to get out of this dress.

Purity's voice turned venomous. "Abel is threatening to publish an exposé on me if I don't sign my contract? That's blackmail!"

Jackson guessed a woman like Purity might have a lot of secrets to hide. Not that he wanted to know any specifics. He just wanted out of here. Oh, he'd always thought of himself as attracted to the wild type. To girls like Annie, the accountant, who'd once worn a zebra-print bodysuit when she'd invited him for dinner. But next to this tigress, Annie looked like a mewling kitten.

"Nobody can pull the wool over my eyes!" Purity shrieked.

Jackson's heart thudded in panic. Had he been found out? No, this statement had ended her phone conversation, which meant he'd have to talk to her. He anxiously watched her stab the off button with a metallic fingernail, then shove the phone into the back pocket of her cutoffs. She strode toward him on those pale well-muscled legs, plopped beside him, then peered in his general direction, through her sunglasses.

"Sorry you had to hear all that," she said, not sounding the least bit apologetic. "It makes me feel so exposed."

Beneath the pink sweater, her breasts spilled from the black leather top, and her milky skin showed through her silver chain necklaces. Before he caught himself, Jackson wistfully murmured, "You *are* exposed...."

"Excuse me?"

Darn! Why had he said that? And how could she not realize he was a man? Quickly raising the pitch of his voice, he continued. "Exposed...because things must be so difficult for you right now." Hoping to sound more housekeeperly, he added, "M' dear."

She didn't seem to notice anything was amiss. She merely nodded as if he'd just confirmed all her own private thoughts. Suddenly reaching out, she squeezed his knee. Jackson ventured a glance down at the long-fingered, slender hand that had just gripped him. His mouth went dry.

"I talked to a woman named Darla," she began.

Sighing shakily as she withdrew her hand, Jackson opened the red pocketbook and withdrew a sheet of paper. Then he panicked. He'd forgotten to take off his watch! It was a man's watch—gold, with a large round face. Well, judging by her taste in clothes, she'd probably think it was a fashion statement. He cleared his throat, which already burned from practicing talking at high pitch. "I have a paper from Darla you'll need to sign...."

He'd go ahead and get the autograph for the poor kid in the hospital. After that, he'd convince Purity to leave Montana. Thrusting a blank sheet in her direction, he handed her a pen.

"This paper is blank," she said.

Jackson's heart skipped a beat. He wished he didn't have to risk talking. His voice wavered in what he could only hope was a feminine way. "Darla needs a signature. Proof I came for the interview...."

She barely seemed to notice him. He guessed it was because he was a servant, and his temper rose. But then Purity took the pen. Using the red pocketbook as a desk, she signed the paper, saying, "And what was your name again?"

Out of habit, he almost said Jackson West. Terror shot through him at the near mistake. If he wasn't careful, he was going to get caught. It would be so embarrassing, he thought, hazarding a glance at the floral jumper. The sheriff was right outside. No doubt there was some law against this ridiculous impersonation.

She sighed. "I just asked for your name."

"Uh..." Scrutinizing her, Jackson suddenly felt paranoid. Did she *really* not know he was a man? Was it possible? His mind raced, trying to think of a name. Hadn't Darla given her one? "Uh...Mrs. Simpson," he finally said. "Mrs. Jean Simpson."

"Right," she said distractedly. "But what am I supposed to call you?"

Jackson was getting darn tired of her tone. "Mrs. Simpson," he said curtly. "Only my *friends* are allowed to call me Jean." Folding her autograph, he made a show of placing it inside the empty pocketbook. But then he couldn't work the catch.

"Here." Purity grabbed the pocketbook, snapped it shut and thrust it back at him. "Don't worry. Everybody gets nervous when they meet celebrities."

Well, wasn't she the cat's meow? Jackson fought not to roll his eyes. Or to tell her that before today he'd never even heard of her or the Trash Cans. Or to say it was no damn wonder she'd wound up paying so much money for this shack. After all, she was awfully liberal with a fountain pen, a blank sheet of paper and her John Hancock.

Whoa, Jackson. He reined in his temper. He guessed what she signed was her business. For a second, he felt torn—should he try to get a corset and follow through on the bet? Or be a good guy and tell her she had to leave?

She said, "I'm so glad you took the job."

He stared at her. He most certainly had not taken this job. Somehow he kept the irony from his tone. "I'm sure you'll want to interview the others...."

For the first time, she looked uncertain. "Uh..." Her

tongue darted out, and she nervously licked her pouty, plum-black lips. "What others?"

Was this a joke? "You know…" The high pitch of Jackson's voice was now from sheer panic. "The others."

"There aren't any others." Purity suddenly wrung her hands. "I needed someone discreet, and Darla said you were the best. She said you're really hard to get because you're in such high demand, but that you'd agreed, because of the salary I'll pay. She said you're the only person she feels I can trust. She said you would never talk to the press. She said…"

He was going to kill Darla. The fury must have shown in his expression.

"It's me!" she suddenly said. "You just don't like my personality. The way I was yelling on the phone, I don't blame you!" Her voice was rising again. "I don't even like myself anymore!"

Oh, please, don't get hysterical. Staring at her sunglasses, Jackson wished he could see her eyes, then maybe he could decide what tack to take with her. "Hmm…" he croaked, reaching for the black sunglasses, "let's take these off…."

He wished he hadn't. Her eyes were as pink and puffy as her sweater. The barely visible irises were brown and the whites were bloodshot. She'd been on a crying jag or a drinking binge. And Jackson devoutly hoped the culprit was liquor. If there was one thing against which he was powerless, it was a woman's tears. He quickly shoved the sunglasses back onto her nose.

But she whipped them right back off again. "No, you're right! I don't have to hide my eyes—or my feelings, anymore!" Her voice climbed with conviction. "Everybody in New York and Hollywood is so fake.

They're all liars and cheats and…'' Her hand slammed down on Jackson's knee again, the grip of her fingers feeling like steel. ''And what I need is to be around good wholesome country people. People like you, Mrs. Simpson.''

Jackson could merely stare. He started to remind her that a wholesome country person had taken her for a ride on this real-estate deal. Staring down at the dress he was wearing, he also wanted to tell her it didn't get any phonier than this. *You've really got to get out of here and out of this dress, Jackson. Forget the corset. Forget the land. You've got the autograph, which'll make that poor kid in the hospital happy.* He cleared his throat. ''Oh, dear, I simply can't take this job….''

''I'll double your salary.''

''Oh, no. It's just—''

''It's me!'' Purity burst out again. ''I *knew* it was me!''

At least she realized she'd made a bad impression, which Jackson guessed was to her credit. ''I'm sorry. I—I like you just fine. But I simply can't…''

''Please!'' she begged.

And then she lunged at his chest. Jackson was so shocked, he felt as if the wind had been knocked out of him. He guessed his ample bosom must have looked maternal, because she locked her arms in a stranglehold around his neck and pressed her head against his heart. Then she started crying. Not little tears, either. But loud, gasping sobs that made her shoulders heave.

''Just don't cry,'' Jackson begged through clenched teeth. ''Please. I'll do anything. Just stop.''

''Please work for me, Mrs. Simpson.''

''Aw, dammit,'' Jackson muttered, feeling furious. ''When do you want me to start?''

"THERE, THERE, m'dear," he crooned.

Jackson's arm had wound up wrapped around her back. Now he surreptitiously tilted his wrist and peeked at his watch. She'd cried for a solid hour now—and he'd felt guiltier by the minute. Even worse, she was still snuggled against him, feeling so warm, soft and heavenly he was in a state of either agony or bliss— he wasn't sure which. But she was a mess—broken-hearted, ditched by her boyfriend and taken advantage of by countless people. Including by him. Her loud-mouthed brassiness was apparently nothing more than a defense mechanism.

It was too bad. It would be a whole lot easier for Jackson to leave a dry-eyed she-devil in the lurch. Should he tell her this was a gag and that he was really a man? After all, she didn't need a cowboy right now. What she needed was womenfolk. If he could just take her up to the ranch, his ma could give her a decent home-cooked meal, and his sisters could offer warmer clothes and plenty of vengeful advice about how to deal with ex-boyfriends.

He sure couldn't take much more of this. He stroked and patted her back while, between sobs, she continued to tell him about her horrible day—how she'd packed the wrong clothes, how it had taken three different air-planes to get to this horrible shack. "And here—" she sniffled, digging deep in her pocket "— look at this."

She tearfully handed him a carefully folded, tiny smudged square, ripped from a newspaper. His heart sank. It was the ad he'd placed in the *Los Angeles Times*. He could barely stand to read it.

Welcome Californians! Come to Miracle Mountain, Montana, and find yourself! This idyllic waterfront cottage hideout is the perfect artist's retreat! Fifty-acre property in private community offers woods, pond, scenic views and more, more, more! Close to skiing, hiking and golf.

"Waterfront," she sniffed.

Jackson carefully refolded the ad and handed it back. Feeling awful, he started to say there *was* a creek out front, but then he thought better of it. Just when he thought he couldn't feel any worse, she hiccuped and said, "You know why I really bought this—" she glanced around. "Cottage?"

He shook his head.

"Because it was in a place called Miracle Mountain. And I could really use a miracle in my life right now." Tears welled in eyes that were so liquid brown and soulful that Jackson's heart hitched. Deep inside him, something hard started to melt. His arm tightened around her back. Damn. The woman had been looking for a miracle and he'd sold her this vermin-ridden shack. Some days he really hated himself.

He learned, between more gasps, that she'd been singing for the Trash Cans for the last five years. Abel Rage, the lead guitar player, had also been her boyfriend until recently. He'd been seeing someone else, and now he was in love and wanted to marry the other woman. Purity was supposed to sign a new contract, and she didn't want to, but Abel Rage was holding some horrible secret over her head, which he threatened to expose if she didn't sign.

Finally, she said defensively, "Well, anyway, I have secrets on Abel, too. He had a drinking problem. I know, because I was his enabler."

Afraid to talk too much, Jackson merely rubbed her back soothingly. The wool of her sweater made his palm itch, making him long to touch her soft-looking skin beneath. But more than that, the sudden exposure of her more sensitive side brought out his protective instincts.

"Enabler?" he prompted.

"You know, I would take care of Abel—get groceries, answer his mail, return his phone calls. It's absolutely the worst thing you can do if someone's drinking."

Jackson frowned. It was? He did all those things for Wyatt Simpson. "Why?"

"It enables them to keep drinking because they don't have to take care of themselves," Purity continued guiltily. "But I didn't know any better at the time. I really thought I was helping." As Purity burrowed against his chest, Jackson tried not to notice how feminine she smelled—all powder and perfume.

"Of course you didn't," Jackson murmured. But he felt terrible. And even guiltier. First, he'd sold this sweet woman a cow camp shack—and now he'd learned that, by trying to help Wyatt, he'd probably been making him even worse.

"Well, I should have known better," Purity said miserably. "Because my own father died..."

Jackson's chest squeezed tight. Could this get any worse? "From drinking?"

She nodded. After a long moment, she said, "And my mother died, too. When I was only twelve."

No wonder she had such a tough, brassy persona. She'd probably fended for herself a lot. And she really must be lonely, to divulge such intimate details to a stranger. He guessed she trusted him because of Darla's recommendation. But what could he do for her? He couldn't really come back here, wearing a dress. She needed girlfriends—*real* girlfriends.

Sitting up bravely, she squared her shoulders and

swiped at her tearstained cheeks. "Sorry, I promise that won't happen again. I'm okay now."

But she wasn't. And Jackson didn't know which touched him more—the sloppy tears or forced bravery. Clearing his throat again, he murmured, "There, m'dear. You just relax and let Mrs. Simpson see what she can do."

Tugging at the jumper hem, Jackson slunk from the room, feeling as low as an earthworm. Fortunately, the old stove was electric and he managed to hook it up. Then he headed outside, and found a fallen tree limb and an ax. Quickly glancing around, he hiked the jumper to his knees, then chopped enough wood to get her through the night. Within a few minutes, a fire was roaring in the old woodstove. Back in the kitchen, he rifled through the cardboard box of supplies she'd brought up from Bozeman. She'd thought to get toilet paper, dishwashing liquid and Ajax, which was good. Otherwise, he didn't recognize half the items. It was all city food. Soy curds and bean threads. Couscous and sun-dried vegetables. Rooting around, he found some herbal tea.

He'd never felt so relieved. In his experience, herbal tea always had a calming effect on women. He washed rust out of an old saucepan and found some tin cups. When the tea was ready, he returned to the living room, crooning, "Now sip this."

And then he stopped in his tracks.

She'd put on round wire-framed granny glasses, and her sincere-looking brown eyes were popping out of her head. *No wonder she didn't know I was a man! She's got bad eyesight!* Jackson tried to still his rapidly beating heart, reminding himself that the sheriff hadn't guessed.

"Don't take this the wrong way," she finally said.

"And it's not that I don't like bright prints, Mrs. Simpson. But I truly think you're tailor-made to wear solids."

Jackson wasn't sure whether he should be relieved or not, but that was exactly what he'd told Darla. This jumper was so bright it could wake the dead. Which, given Mrs. Simpson's real state, he guessed it had. As he crossed the room and handed Purity her tea, he still couldn't believe she really thought he was a woman. Was he going to get away with this charade?

"Have you had your colors done?" she asked conversationally.

Jackson had no idea what she was talking about. He shook his head in what could have been a yes or no.

"Well, you should. I bet you're a summer, which would mean wearing pinks and blues, not reds and oranges." She ventured an apologetic smile. "Sorry, but I always notice clothes. I *love* clothes."

What little you wear of them, Jackson thought, unable to stop his eyes from straying to her black leather corset. "I can see that," he managed dryly.

A long, somewhat awkward silence fell.

"Ah," Purity finally said. "Chamomile tea. Thank you." Suddenly her lower lip trembled and she blinked back fresh tears as if no one had ever done her a kindness. Jackson felt his heart squeeze tight again. Suddenly he wanted to ask her all about herself; about how her parents had died exactly, and about how she'd wound up in a heavy metal band. Not to mention why she needed a miracle in her life.

She glanced around, sighing in shaky relief as she took in the wood-burning stove. "I don't know what I'd do if you couldn't take this job."

Silently Jackson berated himself. The pranks of his youth—stealing from watermelon patches, streaking naked through the town square—had been harmless. This impersonation was not. Purity could be badly hurt. But how was he going to get out of this mess? He watched as she set the tea aside, stood and began pacing again. She looked like her old self. Jackson wasn't sure if that was good or bad.

More to herself than him, she said, "Hmm. I guess we'll have to chop more wood to heat the place. And it's a good thing I bought all that food in Bozeman. There was a sign in the store window saying it was the last real grocery store, though I've no idea what that meant. Well, I guess I can sweep out these leaves and—" She stopped in midpace and squinted around. "Where's the bathroom?"

Jackson winced. "I believe there's just an outhouse."

She stared at him for a long moment, digesting that information. "I'm going to kill Jackson West," she muttered, resuming her pacing. "He's the guy who sold my agent this place."

As if Jackson didn't know. His throat ached from the false soprano, but he raised the pitch of his voice once more, trying to sound chipper. "There *is* a bathtub with running water."

She frowned. "Yeah, right in the middle of the kitchen. I saw that. Well, maybe we can rig up a curtain around it. And get some mousetraps." She shuddered. "Sorry, I just didn't want you to think I was a wimp. But I really do hate mice."

Her gaze flickered over Jackson, as if really seeing him for the first time, and he felt a rush of adrenaline. If she realized he was a man, what would he do? He couldn't tell her he was Jackson West. The woman's opinion of him was already low enough.

He waited, his heart pounding dully. Call it masculine pride, but he half hoped she *would* realize he was a man. He hated to think it was this easy to convince a gorgeous woman he was a female housekeeper.

"Wait a minute," she finally said. "How old are you?"

Realizing he'd been holding his breath, Jackson slowly exhaled. He had no idea what she was guessing—fifty or sixty, maybe. "Uh…a woman never tells."

She glanced around grimly and said, "I don't know how to chop wood, but I don't want you to strain yourself. And I guess the walls in here need to be fixed…."

Jackson had to fight not to say "Hallelujah." Here was his out. "Of course not, m'dear. But I have an able-bodied son…"

Purity shook her head. "No men." Her expression turned flinty. "Especially not able-bodied ones."

Jackson didn't know what compelled him to dig for information—her need to unburden herself or his male curiosity. "Because of what Abel did?"

Purity shrugged, suddenly looking distant. "I guess."

Well, he could hardly come over with his toolbox and introduce himself as Jackson West. If he did, she'd probably run him off the property with the rifle in the corner. Lifting a wrist, Jackson let it go limp. "But my son, uh, Wyatt…why, he's harmless as a fly. He can fix insulation, hook up the remaining appliances, check the wiring…."

Purity looked stricken. "Well…how old is he?"

This would work. He could come, introduce himself as Wyatt and make the place habitable. "Thirty-three."

Purity pulled the open sides of her pink sweater together. "Oh, I don't know about this."

Jackson frowned. The woman wore underwear as

outerwear, and sang for crowds on a stage. Judging from her phone conversation, she didn't think twice about delivering tongue-lashings. Surely she could handle a cowpoke with a toolbox. Jackson didn't understand the problem. Nevertheless he tried to conjure an image of a man who was totally harmless—which meant the complete opposite of himself.

"My Wyatt never drinks, gambles or womanizes. He's a good, Christian boy. And he could come right up tonight, in two shakes of a lamb's tail."

"In two shakes of a lamb's tail?" Purity said nervously.

"Why, that's just country talk for in a hurry."

"I don't mean to be rude—but he'd leave me alone?"

Jackson's gaze drifted over her. *Probably not.* "Of course."

"But *you'll* come in the morning?" she said quickly.

"Oh, you won't need me again. Wyatt can take care of everything...." Jackson's voice trailed off. Those damnable tears were clinging in her eyelashes again. Shoot, he'd sold her this horrible shack. He guessed it wouldn't kill him to come back dressed this way, just once more. By tomorrow she'd be settled and he could resign as Mrs. Simpson. "All right." Even as he said it, Jackson wished the floor would open and swallow him.

"I still don't feel entirely comfortable about having your son come. You see..." Purity sat next to Jackson and took his hand, as if she meant to make a serious confession. For a second he felt breathless. Was she going to divulge the horrible secret with which Abel Rage was blackmailing her?

Jackson never found out, because touching his hands derailed Purity's thought and she said, "Oh, Mrs.

Simpson, your hands are so rough!'' She darted across the room, and urgently rifled through her bags as if rough skin were a malady akin to the plague. Returning with a black-and-gold jar, she said, ''Here. We'd better try this cream. It's Chanel. It's very good.''

Having no choice but to appear grateful, Jackson dutifully unscrewed the dainty canister and slapped cream onto his hands.

''Oh, no,'' Purity protested, her voice still throaty from crying. ''You need to rub it in much more gently. Here, let me show you.''

Jackson had never known hand-holding could be so sensual. Purity lathered the lotion all over his left hand. Making a fist, she lightly pounded the back of the hand, then she threaded her fingers through his, working them outward. After that, she turned his hand over. Holding it palm up, she massaged with her thumbs. When she was done, she placed his left hand on her bare knee and then started on his other hand.

''Your hands are incredibly strong,'' she murmured.

Jackson could barely find his voice. His hands were nowhere near as strong as the dreamy sensual feelings aroused by her massage. ''Oh, I work in the garden, m'dear,'' he managed to say faintly. He could hardly tell her he spent ten hours a day on horseback, with his hands threaded through leather reins.

''And these calluses,'' she murmured. ''We'll have to work on these.''

Jackson sighed. Why did she have to be so sweet? And smell like a basket of flowers? He wanted to tug off his wig, draw her gently into his arms and kiss her senseless. He wanted to feel her crushed against his chest—his *real* chest.

''We'll start every morning with a hand massage,'' she promised. ''I bet we can get rid of these calluses.''

She sighed and her eyes settled on his. "And maybe we can paint your nails."

"No!" Jackson said in a voice deeper than he'd intended.

"Sorry, Mrs. Simpson. I..." Her gaze drifted guiltily over him. "Of course you wouldn't want painted nails. You're so practical and sensible. I bet you never even wear high heels." Her cheeks colored. "You must think I look...*garish,* huh?"

Jackson shook his head in quick denial.

"C'mon. Be honest. Woman to woman."

Everything in her eyes demanded his response. "Uh...that black lipstick might be a *little* harsh," he finally offered.

She squinted back, as if the thought had never occurred to her. "Hmm," she finally said, "I bet your son really is a good Christian man."

Jackson winced. He hadn't seen the inside of the local church since his father's funeral fifteen years ago. And Wyatt Simpson, the real Wyatt Simpson, was a no-account drunk—one Jackson now knew he'd probably enabled and made worse. Somehow Jackson nodded. "Oh, yes. A *very* good Christian."

She looked almost convinced.

Jackson bit back a sigh. If he didn't figure out a way to come up here and make the place habitable, she'd stay in it just the way it was—mice and all. And he could hardly fix the insulation wearing calf-length jumpers. Clearing his aching throat once more, he said, "I'm Wyatt's mother, so I'm no judge. But I don't think he's—" Jackson forced himself to wince sadly "—considered too handsome. Oh, of course, he's handsome to me, since I'm his mama...."

"And he can spend tonight here?"

Jackson's breath caught. Was she afraid to stay here alone? Did she want company? ''All night?''

''No, just this evening! Of course not all night!''

Disappointment flooded him, but trying to sound scandalized, Jackson gasped, ''My Wyatt would never think of such a thing!''

3

BE CAREFUL. He's going to turn around any second and catch you staring. Purity hunkered down, peeking between the slats of the new blinds in the bedroom spying, as she had been all week, on the man who'd come up here and introduced himself as Wyatt Simpson. Like most mothers, Mrs. Simpson completely lacked objectivity when it came to her only son. The man had turned out to be a superhunk. *Don't be such a wuss. Just go out there and talk to him.* But only her eyes moved, drifting over him. And her stomach, which fluttered with butterflies.

Even though the air was chilly, his faded blue denim work shirt was hanging on a log protruding from the woodpile, along with his tan Western-style hat. He was dressed only in cowboy boots and threadbare jeans that clung to his lower body, molding every contour, and the sunlight that poured over his bare bronzed back danced in the waves of sun-streaked hair that almost touched his shoulders. Mesmerized by his rippling muscles, Purity watched him grab a log and upend it on a tree stump. Widening his stance, he brought the ax down with a whack, easily splitting the wood.

What a man. "He's like all those Marlboro guys rolled into one," she whispered. *And he's turning around!* Her neck retracted like a scared turtle's and she hunched her shoulders as if ducking a blow, crouching down even further. The front of him was as enticing as the back. Everything—from his flat, sun-coppered belly, to the thatch of golden hair between his pectorals—conjured images of thick, hay-colored ropes, leather chaps, denim and horses. He was all-economy, with nothing wasted—just tanned skin stretched taut over sharp bones and rock-hard muscles. She doubted she could pinch an inch of flesh anywhere on him.

He had a craggy cowboy face, with fine laugh lines deepening the corners of squinty eyes that were the same dreamy blue as his mother's. In fact, their eyes were so much alike, they could have been the same person. The son's glistening white teeth flashed with easy smiles, and his good temperament was always evident since—like his mother—he had a habit of whistling old campfire ditties when he thought no one was within earshot. As "Home on the Range" segued into "Oh Susannah," he headed for the woodpile again on his long, rangy legs. Purity loved watching the slow, sexy roll of his gait. Even though his feet were firmly planted on the ground, he always looked as if he were riding a horse, rather than walking.

And he was nice.

That was the real killer. Because his poor mom had only been able to come a couple of times before she'd been taken ill with the flu, Wyatt had worked doubly hard to help make the shack habitable. He'd set up a table in the living room, and brought her a feather mattress from home, which he'd tossed across her double bed. Drywall now covered the previously exposed insulation, the appliances were operable and she had new blinds. After he'd installed a toilet and enclosed it with a makeshift wall, he'd attached a shower nozzle to the bathtub, around which he'd rigged a curtain. Then he'd brought her a TV from the Sears in Silver Spoon, and warmer clothes—some jeans and sweatshirts.

In their brief, awkward conversations, he'd told her he worked for Jackson West. But when she told him Jackson had sold her this miserable place, Wyatt swore Jackson was a nice guy, that there must have been a misunderstanding. She doubted it. Obviously, Mrs. Simpson's poor son put in long, hard hours as a ranch hand and, judging from his and his mother's home, which was visible right down the hill, Jackson wasn't paying Wyatt nearly enough. Yeah, she fumed, she had Jackson West's number. He was taking advantage of Wyatt. At first, the sweet cowboy wouldn't even accept money for the work he was doing here. From sheer nervousness over Wyatt's blond, blue-eyed good looks, she'd wound up yelling her head off before she'd gotten him to take the envelopes of cash she now left for him on the kitchen counter. The whole time they'd argued, she was sure she'd faint from a panic attack.

But he deserved the money. He'd even insisted on giving her rudimentary survival lessons. Even now, she could feel how he'd nestled himself behind her, wrapping his arms tightly around her waist as he showed her how to split logs. Later, as he'd coached her on shooting the rifle, he'd kept calling her ''sugar'' in a sexy drawl. She thought she'd swoon—either from the voice, or from how the hard wall of his chest pressed against her.

''Ready, aim, fire,'' he'd whispered.

''Shoot.'' She sighed dreamily now, remembering how the rifle's kick sent her reeling backward, into his arms. She could have died happily, right then and there.

So, go out and talk to him, you wuss! He's just a man. That means he's exactly like a woman—only different. So what if he has chest hair? A deeper voice?

A completely different anatomy? Feeling woozy, she sagged against the window frame. No, she couldn't go out there.

"But I'm out of food," she whispered miserably.

Even worse, she needed Tampax. Should she creep out and leave her grocery list on the counter for him? Somehow she simply couldn't imagine sending this cowboy to the store for Tampax.

"You don't have a choice." If only she knew when his mother was coming back...

But she didn't. So she'd just have to conjure up her alter ego. She'd simply charge right out there in her combat boots and bellow, "I need you to go to the store right now." Then she'd shove the grocery list in the sexy man's hand, stomp loudly back into the bedroom and slam the door. No big deal.

Her only other option was to brave the great outdoors, herself, which meant facing the sheriff's roadblock. Not to mention driving the Land Rover again. She'd managed to get it here from Bozeman, but she wasn't a very good driver. No one drove in New York, and she hadn't been in L.A. very long.

Taking a deep breath, she glanced down at her outfit—oversize jeans and a navy sweatshirt. She'd pared down her nails and changed her polish and lipstick to a light pink, thinking Wyatt might like that better. He was so cute. *Puh-lease. The man doesn't even know you exist! Every time he comes over, you hide in the bedroom!*

She glanced nervously toward the dresser where she'd laid out the shopping list. She'd rewritten it countless times, in case she really did wind up giving it to Wyatt. She just couldn't stand the thought of him seeing her messy handwriting. *Oh, what's wrong with you? He's a cowboy, not an English teacher. He's not going to grade you on the penmanship of your grocery list!*

Suddenly Wyatt turned around again. Dropping the blind, Purity leapt back as if she'd been burned. Had he seen her? Leaning against the wall, she pressed her hand to her rapidly beating heart. "He saw me," she whispered. "I know he did."

And then she heard a door close.

He's coming back inside! Was he going to confront her? To ask her why she kept spying on him?

She really couldn't stand this tension. Her life could not have been more dramatic if there was a serial killer in her cabin, instead of a cute cowboy.

"It's okay," she whispered. "He doesn't know the truth about me."

And she really hoped Abel Rage wouldn't tell the press the deep, dark secret he was holding over her head. That she, Purity—sexy, provocative, worldly-wise lead singer of the Trash Cans and grist for the tabloid mill—was really an alter ego for plain old Ellen Smith. Even though she was about to turn thirty, she was still impossibly shy—at least if she was within a mile radius of an attractive Y chromosome.

And even worse, she was still a virgin.

ANOTHER HOUR HAD PASSED.

And Purity was starting to feel very tired of being cooped up in her bedroom. She paused, her hand on the doorknob. "Okay," she whispered, "I have everything." The grocery list was neatly folded in her hand. Her phone was tucked into the back pocket of her jeans. She was wearing her combat boots, plenty of earrings, and since she was only slightly nearsighted, she was leaving her glasses behind. She drew a deep breath and slowly exhaled. *Ready or not, here I come.*

She flung open the door and clomped toward the kitchen. Her voice was strong, forceful. "Wyatt? Is that you, Wyatt?"

Still bare-chested, but now wearing his Stetson, he was lounging casually against the counter. At first, he didn't respond, as if he were used to answering to some other name. But then he turned around, smiling. "Who else would it be?"

Just that low gravelly drawl was enough to stop her in her tracks. No matter how much she wanted to edge around the bathtub and approach him, all her limbs became instantly stiff, as if wooden splints had been strapped to all her joints. She managed to shrug. "I don't know. Maybe your mother."

He shook his head. "Just me. Haven't seen you lately, sugar."

Her heart was hammering hard against her ribs. Coming out here was a very bad idea. Could she say "Hi," whirl around and storm back to the bedroom again? She slicked her damp palms down the sides of her jeans.

He was watching her with the bemused expression he always wore when he saw her. "What have you been up to?"

Oh, you know. Rewriting my grocery list for you in various print and cursive styles. She pointed her thumb toward the bedroom. "Working. Writing some songs." She'd attempted a strident tone, which meant her register was too loud and that her damnably deep, rich voice was making the flimsy walls of the shack tremble. She forced herself to continue. "And I...just came out because I was wondering when your mother is coming back. I mean..."

He raised a bushy, golden blond eyebrow.

Remember, you're the employer here. "I know she

was ill, but she was hired to do a job. She was supposed to be here on a daily basis. And I need..." She sounded so insensitive! And nothing could be further from the truth. She was extremely worried about Mrs. Simpson's flu.

His voice was a soft drawl. "What do you need?"

You. The thought came unbidden. Unwanted heat crept into her cheeks and there wasn't a damn thing she could do about it. Even worse, she was fairly sure he was attracted to her. No doubt he was a good Christian man, just as his mother had said. But he was still a man. To his credit, he was trying not to stare, but those cornflower blue eyes did keep drifting.

Just pretend you're on stage. "For one..." Her vocal register was still excruciating, but she forged ahead. "I need groceries. And...and well, I'm worried about your mother." She couldn't help it. Because she was nervous, her voice was continuing to rise in both pitch and tempo. "She's been sick for nearly a week! Are you sure it's the flu? I mean, what kind of flu lasts a week?" *Oh, what am I rambling about? And I still sound so heartless.* "I'd better go down and see her." She glanced back toward the bedroom. "Yes, that's what I'll do. I'll get my jacket right now—"

"No." He quickly shook his head. "It could be contagious. I'm sure you need to protect your voice, and her symptoms include a sore throat. So maybe you should just give me a grocery list. I'll make sure you get everything you need."

She hated the pleading tone that crept into her voice. "I...I'd rather give it to your mother."

He squinted at her as if not understanding her problem. "But I'm more than happy to pick up groceries for you."

Grow up. Just give him the damn list. This was

crazy. She'd lived in New York City for nearly ten years. Her deep voice had terrorized muggers, irritable cabbies and unsavory characters in countless smoke-filled clubs. Unfortunately this particular cowboy didn't even seem to notice it. "Fine," she huffed.

She started toward him, the taps of her combat boots clanking on the bare wood floor. She nearly made it—she was only a pace away—when she tripped and lunged right at Wyatt. In midair, she decided she probably should have worn her glasses. Only his rock-hard midsection kept her from falling on her face. Her right cheek wound up pressed flat against his suntanned belly, her ear right over his navel, as if she'd mistaken it for a seashell and was now trying to hear the call of the ocean. What she heard was the call of the wild. His work-roughened hand caught her elbow, steadied her, then hauled her to an upright position.

"I'm…" *Mortified.* Somehow she tamped down the color threatening to flood her cheeks. Feeling the pulse ticking in her throat, she glanced over him. "Are you all right?"

His soft chuckle further unnerved her. "Sugar, I'm twice your size. I think I'll live."

"I just asked if you were all right," she managed coolly. "It was just a question. Okay?"

"Okay." His lips quirked, and his tanned hand absently rubbed his belly, touching the spot where her ear had been and ruffling the few golden hairs that narrowed toward his thick brown leather belt and jeans waistband. "So, do you want the real answer?"

Her heart skipped a beat. "Did I hurt you? Oh, no. I really did hurt you, didn't I?"

He grinned. "Well, the imprint of all those earrings might be embedded in me for life," he said, his voice serious. "But I swear, I won't sue."

Now he was making fun of her. "I said I was sorry," she began. "I promise, I don't usually trip. I'm extremely well coordinated and physical. You probably wouldn't guess it, because I haven't been working out since I got here, but I usually exercise regularly and..." She realized her head was starting to bob up and down defensively. "And I..." And she what? Her mind raced. "And you wouldn't believe how much I can bench-press." *I can't believe I just said that.*

His lips were twitching furiously. "You promise you don't usually trip? Cross your heart and hope to die?"

Don't make fun of me. Her temper flared.

He said, "Can I ask you something?"

She hoped it was something easy—like how much weight she could lift. The answer was: enough to knock him right off his feet. She managed to wave her hand carelessly in the air. "Uh, feel free to ask me anything at all."

He was staring at her. "I make you nervous, don't I?"

She forced herself to stare right back, but now she felt as if her eyes were bugging in her head. She probably looked like Marty Feldman. "What?"

"I said, do I—"

"I heard you!"

Suddenly, something shrill sounded. It was close by, and because her nerves were so on edge, she actually jumped and let out a yelp.

Very carefully he said, "That was the phone in your back pocket. It's ringing."

She stamped her foot. "I know that!"

He put his hands up, as if she were arresting him, and his voice was so calm, he could have been dealing with a mental patient. "Of course you did."

But she hadn't. This cowboy had tangled up her

nerves so badly that she couldn't think straight. She was furious with herself. Which was good. When she was angry, her man shyness vanished. Glad for the diversion, she whipped out her telephone and answered it. It was Abel. He'd already called three times today.

"Cut me a break, Abel," she shouted in a rush. "I just need some space. I want to think about my life. Why won't you leave me alone and let me call you in a few days?" As usual, he wouldn't listen. "Abel, *puhlease.*"

She didn't know if it was good or bad, but Mrs. Simpson's son's hand closed over hers. As he eased the phone from her death grip, a shiver of heat zipped up her spine.

"Abel," he said in a soft, honeyed drawl, "Purity doesn't want to talk to you right now."

This cowboy had unnerved her, but she couldn't help feeling pleased. Abel might think twice about revealing her sexual inexperience to the press if he knew she was entertaining a man in an idyllic Montana cottage retreat. She glanced around. Well, okay, so it wasn't idyllic. But Abel didn't know that. She stared at Wyatt, feeling another rush of warmth wash over her. Oh, maybe she should have been angry about the way he'd horned in on her phone call, but she wasn't.

He covered the mouthpiece. "Abel says he knows you're not really mad about him breaking up with you. And that you don't know how to have fun anymore." A heartbeat passed and Wyatt added, "Who am I? I'm a friend."

Even though Wyatt was still less than a foot away, Purity's respiration was slowing. But she was starting to get ticked off at Abel. "Well, you tell Abel he should grow up. There's a lot more to life than fun."

"Abel," he drawled, "the lady says life's not all beer 'n' skittles."

Purity squinted. Had she said that? She guessed "beer 'n' skittles" was akin to "fun and games."

He covered the mouthpiece again. "He says you're a real trip."

She rolled her eyes. "He's such an egotist."

"Abel, she says you're gettin' too big for your britches," he said into the receiver.

Purity's lips twitched with the first real merriment she'd felt in ages. Abel was originally from the Bronx. He dressed exclusively in black leather, had a pierced eyebrow and four tattoos, and she was sure no one had ever spoken to him as Wyatt was now.

Suddenly his whole body became more alert—the muscles of his bare chest tensing, his eyes darkening to an angry midnight blue—and the changes in him made her pulse accelerate. Shooting her a protective glance, he covered the mouthpiece again. "Abel says he's going to…expose you for what you really are."

"Tell him he can't! He just can't!" Oh, the Trash Cans weren't a huge band. But they'd cut records and played a lot of New York clubs. Everybody thought she was…so experienced. No thirty-year-old virgin would want her sexual status announced in *Music Beat* or *Rolling Stone*. Especially not one with a flamboyant man-eating persona. As things stood, she was rumored to have slept with half the men in Hollywood.

Warring emotions crossed the sexy cowboy's features, curiosity among them. She swallowed hard. Heaven only knew what he thought her deep dark secret was. He probably thought she'd robbed banks or something.

"Mess with her," he warned, talking to Abel again, "and you'll mess with me."

"Wow," Purity whispered in awe, her heart fluttering. This was right out of the movies. Suddenly she imagined Abel chasing her with a posse, then Wyatt galloping past on a horse, sweeping her off her feet. She clutched the mane while a strong arm snaked around her waist.

"Abel says he's sorry. He'll wait for you to call him."

As Wyatt turned off the phone, Purity blinked, his voice transporting her back from the Wild West to the kitchen of the shack. She beamed at him. She'd been shrieking at both Abel and her manager for days. Why did no one ever listen to her? *My hero,* she thought. "Thanks, Wyatt," she said. "I mean it."

"Now, sugar, why don't you give me that shopping list?"

It was still folded in her hand. She was so mesmerized by him, that she simply handed it over. "Please," she suddenly said in panic, realizing her mistake, "couldn't you give it to your mother?"

But he was already reading it. "Six pomegranates. Four mangoes. Couscous, Somen noodles, Somen Tsyu sauce…" He sighed and glanced up, his blue eyes settling apologetically on hers. He slowly drawled, "Sorry, sugar, but the only thing our general store is gonna have is your Tampax. Now, you wrote Tampax twice. Was that a mistake or did you need two boxes?"

The longer the silence stretched, the more ridiculous she felt. *By the time they're my age, most women have been married for ten years! They've had children! They don't feel embarrassed about things such as this!* Oh, why did she have to be so excruciatingly, painfully shy around men she was seriously attracted to? As usual, her voice was twice as loud as she intended. "Uh…one box is fine, Wyatt. Now, if you'll just excuse me."

She edged back toward the bedroom.

But he was following her. "Which should I get?" he said. "Regular? Super? Super-Plus? What?"

"Regular," she managed to whisper. And then she turned and fled. God only knew what he thought about the wild, trapped gleam he'd no doubt seen in her eyes. After a long moment, there was a knock on the bedroom door.

"Uh, Purity?"

She blew out a shaky breath, feeling like a fool. "Hmm?"

"Did I say something wrong? Are you all right in there?"

"I'm fine. I just…need to get back to writing my songs. You know, I'm under deadlines here!" She'd never written a song in her life. Abel wrote all the music for the Trash Cans. All she could do was sing. She stared at the door, praying Wyatt's footsteps would retreat.

"Uh…I guess I'll just leave for the day. And…would it be better if I sent my mother back with the groceries? I, uh, think she might be feeling better now."

Relief flooded her. She'd desperately wanted to get to know Mrs. Simpson's son, Wyatt, but now she was so embarrassed by her own self-consciousness that she really didn't want to see him again. "Your mother? Oh, that would be great!"

"Mrs. Simpson?" Purity called from the kitchen. "Is that you? Wyatt said he wouldn't be back today. C'mon in! Are you feeling better?"

Jackson didn't know what to make of it. One minute, she was speechless. And the next, she was talking a blue streak. Even worse, he was still having trouble remembering to respond to the names "Mrs. Simpson" and "Wyatt." For once, he'd like to hear the woman call him by his real name. On his way to the kitchen, Jackson saw a towel folded on a stool and he hesitated, adjusting the grocery bags on his hips. She was in the bathtub. If he did the gentlemanly thing and left, the ice cream would melt.

His eyes trailed over the lace curtain. She hadn't drawn the heavier shower liner behind it, and light shone through the lace. He could see the silhouette of her upswept hair and slender neck, and the fragrance of her soap—oranges and vanilla—hung in the air. Averting his gaze, Jackson felt warring emotions. Sure, he wanted to look. Hell, he wanted to climb right in the tub with her. But he was here under false pretenses, so anything other than matronly attention didn't seem fair. And when he was pretending to be Wyatt, he was supposed to be a good Christian.

"I'm so glad you're feeling better!" she exclaimed.

The genuine relief in her voice touched him. Heading for the counter, he mustered his best falsetto. "Thank you, m'dear."

"You still sound a little throaty, though."

"Hmm…yes."

At least she wasn't bathing right in front of him. As soon as he could, he'd head back to the ranch. Jackson would have come and gone by now, if he hadn't decided to press a solid, light blue jumper. Ironing the countless pleats had made his hands hurt worse than a set of reins ever could, and he'd burned his thumb. How women managed, he'd never know.

Setting Purity's shopping list on the counter, he decided she had the most practiced penmanship he'd ever seen. And suddenly he recalled his father saying that neat handwriting was the mark of a good woman, since it showed a well-ordered mind. Jackson hadn't thought about that for years. As he put away the groceries, a low note sounded from behind the shower curtain, and he realized he'd been whistling "Oh Susannah."

"Oh, please," she said cheerfully. "Keep whistling."

He did. And she began singing the words with a voice that was deep and rich with emotion. He let it warm him as he thought about this crazy week. After Purity had indirectly informed him that he was enabling Wyatt Simpson's drinking, Jackson had called the therapist he'd dated in Silver Spoon.

Sure enough, she'd agreed. Jackson *was* an enabler. She'd referred him to the psychiatric ward of the hospital, where he was told there was only one option. Since he owned the house in which Wyatt was living, he had to turn Wyatt into the street, unless Wyatt agreed to enter a twenty-eight day rehabilitation program for alcoholism.

Wyatt—the real Wyatt—was furious. But the young man was now in the hospital, where hopefully they'd break down his anger and get him sober. At least Jackson felt good about that. And good about how happy he'd heard Purity's autograph had made the little girl, who was in the same hospital. Still, between the ranch and Purity, Jackson was running himself ragged.

Purity. If he didn't know better, he'd think she'd been embarrassed about asking him to pick up Tampax. But that was impossible. Hell, he had three sisters and they didn't think twice about it. Besides, she was a city girl and big-time singer. He was flattering himself, if he really thought some backwoods cowboy was going to rattle her cage. Still, she seemed to have one personality when Jackson pretended to be Mrs. Simpson, and another when he pretended to be Wyatt. When she splashed in the water behind him, he fought the urge to turn around.

"Did they have all my stuff at the store?"

Jackson cleared his throat. "Only Tampax. Sorry, m'dear. But Wyatt got some sweet potatoes and nice juicy steaks." When there was no response, he could have kicked himself. She was from California. She was probably a vegetarian. "Is that all right?"

Just as he turned around, she whipped back the lace curtain. His breath caught. God, she was beautiful. She was nestled neck-deep in bubbles; damp tendrils of platinum hair curled against her cheeks, which were rosy from the hot water. He wanted to say that she was the first goddess he'd ever encountered who was wearing granny glasses.

"You're *definitely* a summer," she said.

Jackson glanced down at the light blue jumper he was wearing. "Thanks."

"Steaks," she enthused with a nod, pressing her glasses more firmly to the bridge of her nose, then raising a well-toned arm and washing it gently with a cloth. "Well, you'll have to show me how to cook them. I usually only eat them in restaurants, because I don't know how." She beamed up at him beatifically. "I'd like to learn, though! I love a good steak."

She was chattering on as if Jackson's whole world hadn't ground to a halt at the sight of her.

"In fact," she continued, "I love to put ketchup on my steaks. Oh, I know it's totally outré."

His throat was bone-dry. "Outré?"

"You know, gauche. Tacky. Would you be highly offended if I put ketchup on my steaks, Mrs. Simpson?"

His eyes drifted over her. The tiny drying bubbles on her shoulders caught the light, like prisms. He could barely find his voice. "Really, you can do anything you want. Absolutely anything."

"Great. And, Mrs. Simpson...?"

"Hmm?"

Her voice caught with concern. "There's something weird on my back. Could you please look at it? Would you mind?"

How could he say no?

Sensing his hesitation, she glanced up. And then she grinned. "Mrs. Simpson," she chided softly, "we're all girls here! Now, c'mon."

Jackson edged around the bathtub. When Purity wiggled upward and craned her head around, he became aware of the heat of her body, and of how her breath teased his cheek. But that took a back seat to his concern. "Hold still," he murmured. "It's just a mild rash. But we'd better get you to a dermatologist down in Silver Spoon." Fortunately, he'd dated one last winter, and they'd parted on good terms. Should he call her?

"Is it little red blistery things?" she said.

He frowned. "Yeah."

She shrugged. "I always get that. I have very fine skin."

She sure did. And his hands suddenly longed to touch every inch of it. No woman had ever affected him like this. His chest squeezed tight with the realization that it wasn't just her looks. Oh, she was beautiful. Maybe the most beautiful woman he'd ever seen. But she was so unguarded right now. So at ease in the company of her housekeeper. He'd never seen a woman look so...totally herself.

And then it hit Jackson like a bolt of lightning. *It's because she thinks I'm a woman.* Dressed in jeans and a Stetson, he really did make her nervous. The thought made his heart ache, since he'd never wanted to make her—or any woman—anxious. Of course, dressed in Mrs. Simpson's clothes, he wasn't quite himself, either. Was he more attentive? More thoughtful? More *sensitive?*

She sent him a sweet, apologetic smile. "Mind handing me that towel, so I won't drip on your nice clean floor?"

Still reeling from the revelation that his male presence unbalanced her, he grabbed the towel. Shaking it open, he held it out. Just as he did, a great splash sounded—and she rose right out of the water.

Everything seemed to stop—his breath, his steps, his heart.

Before he knew it, she'd spun around and he was wrapping the towel around her back. Less than a second had passed. But he'd seen her—every blessed inch. Her high, firm breasts were too full for his hands, and her sweet pale belly was curved, her hips round. Her backside was something out of his most secret dreams.

Oblivious to what she was doing to him, she said, "If I go get my robe, would you mind doing my hands? You know, the way I do yours?"

Numbly Jackson nodded. And then he headed for the table in the living room. When she emerged from her bedroom, she was belting a black silk robe. She seated herself across from him, then reached and squeezed his hands.

"It's so good to see you again, Mrs. Simpson. I was worried sick. Wyatt said you were highly contagious, and that I shouldn't visit because of my voice." She sighed. "He's so thoughtful."

Thoughtful? Jackson managed a smile as he unscrewed the lid of the hand cream canister. He was unsure of himself but he did his best. He rubbed in a tiny dollop of the cream, threaded his fingers through hers and worked them outward. Then he turned her hand over and began a deep massage of her palm.

She shut her eyes and moaned. "Ah...you're so strong. It makes you so good at this."

Her voice thrummed through him. Shutting his own eyes, Jackson deeply massaged, enjoying the touch of her—so sensual but not sexual. It made him want to brush her hair and paint her toenails. After a long moment, he opened his eyes again.

She was smiling.

He smiled back.

"My real name's Ellen," she suddenly said softly. "Ellen Smith."

Jackson's lips parted in surprise. Purity's real name was plain old Ellen Smith? Every moment with this woman was a revelation. He chuckled softly, then remembered he needed to watch his voice. Raising it to a soprano register, he said, "Would you rather be called Ellen?"

"You know—" she sounded surprised "—I think I would."

"Ellen," he said, liking the simple sound of the name.

A blissful, comfortable silence fell.

Still smiling, Jackson wished he could share a moment like this with her when he was dressed in jeans and a hat. And then his gaze settled on a brown paper bag of clothes in the corner. The black, silver-studded corset on top suddenly, intrusively, reminded Jackson of the real reason he was here—to win a fool bet. He frowned.

"Oh," she murmured. "It would be great if you could take those things to the trash, Mrs. Simpson. They're either too small or torn or..." She shrugged.

"I'm beginning to think I want some new clothes that are less risqué."

Jackson titled his head, considering. The corsets were a turn-on, no doubt about it. But she was adorable in baggy jeans and a sweatshirt. "You look great in anything," he couldn't help but say as he lifted her hand again and rubbed in another dollop of cream.

"Thanks."

He nodded and continued massaging.

After a long time, she sighed. "You know, I grew up in a small town in Oklahoma. Because my mother died when I was young, and then my father started drinking, I never had anybody to talk to. So I never really knew how to handle myself...."

When Jackson glanced up, a lock of gray wig hair swung against his cheek and he brushed it away. Probably if he was dressed in his jeans and cowboy hat, he'd end the conversation right here. This was girl talk. But he was dressed as Mrs. Simpson. And, he liked listening to Ellen confide. Even if he had no idea what had prompted these thoughts, or where she was headed.

"And?"

She smiled wanly. "Well, I developed early, and the way the guys would look at me scared me to death. I...sort of had this look-but-don't-touch aura. Guys used to call me the Ice Princess." Jackson's eyes drifted over her face. Deep inside, he felt a twinge of guilt. He'd teased girls about being ice princesses in the past. "You're a beautiful girl."

Her smile was easy. "Thanks."

Jackson's breath caught again. Her response lacked the coy glance that usually accompanied reactions to his compliments. And he liked this easy acceptance of his admiration. Liked the way she'd responded when she didn't realize the compliment was from a man.

Another comfortable silence fell, and a feeling of deep contentment stole over Jackson. Oh, he'd always felt relaxed around women, but he'd never managed to be friends with any of them. It wasn't all his fault it never happened, either. Women fussed over him, cooked, ironed his shirts—when all along, he was craving good, honest conversation. But once sex entered the picture, a man became a man. And a woman, a woman. And there was so much "push-me, pull-me" that Jackson had never had much luck winding up equal partners, much less real friends.

Of course, it was his fault, too. Casual flirtation came easily to him. Not so, talking about his feelings. But right now, with Ellen thinking he was a woman, he figured he should start trying harder. Because he could see a flicker of what a good friendship with a woman like Ellen could be. It glimmered in front of him like a star in the big Montana sky he loved.

Ellen suddenly sighed. "Because I was so shy, Mrs. Simpson, I never wound up going out with guys."

Now *that* he couldn't believe. Jackson raised his eyebrows.

"Oh, I tried in high school." A hint of anger touched her voice. "But I guess—because of the way I looked—they all wanted to brag about their conquests with me. Supposedly I'd slept with all these guys at school...."

"And you didn't?" Later, he guessed she'd loosened up. He'd read about her exploits in Darla's fanzines.

She shook her head. "No. That my father drank didn't help. I was vulnerable." She glanced around with a sudden wry smile. "It's years with that man that makes me not think twice about staying in a place like this. Living with an alcoholic, you learn to make quick adjustments—for good and bad. Anyway, the guys I wanted to know in high school were only out for one thing.''

"There must have been one nice guy."

"I didn't meet him."

Jackson's heart stretched to breaking. Real pain had edged into her voice. He could have kicked himself for every time he'd kissed and told. Or lied. "Guys can be mean."

She grimaced. "Aren't they just awful, Mrs. Simpson?"

That might be taking it a little far. Jackson had a sudden, almost desperate urge to show her a man could be wonderful, and a crazy plan formed in his head: to use what he'd learned about her today to help make her less shy around him, as a man. His eyes traced over her creamy skin and light hair, noticing how it was offset by her brown eyes and the delicate mole by her lip. "So…what's this secret Abel's holding over your head?" Maybe he could help.

"You promise you'll never tell anyone?"

He hesitated. Should he agree? If she'd done something criminal, he'd have to take the promise back and turn her in. Finally he nodded his head.

She whispered, "I'm a virgin."

His hand tightened reflexively on hers. She couldn't be serious. With looks like hers, surely some man had…

"I know it's a shock," she said, as if reading his mind. "According to the fanzines, I've slept around a lot." Her voice rose angrily. "But…reporters lie as much as those guys back in high school."

He couldn't believe it. "But you dated Abel?"

She sighed. "The only reason I was able to go out with him for so long was because I wasn't very attracted to him. I mean, I do love him. But as a friend.

In fact, he might be the one nice guy I know, and even though I was mad at first, I couldn't be happier that he's found someone. He never made me nervous, though, the way men do if I'm attracted. And...you know how you kiss a guy, Mrs. Simpson?''

Jackson didn't have a clue. And he was still stunned by the fact that her nervousness might mean she was attracted to him. He managed to nod.

"And the kiss is right or it's not?" she continued.

Now that, Jackson knew about. He nodded again.

"Well, Abel was just too...mushy with his lips."

Jackson winced. Lordy, did women really talk this way in closed company? He must have looked shocked, because Ellen rushed on. "Oh, I almost slept with him anyway. I admit it's wrong, since we weren't really in love, but I wanted to know what it was like." She was getting agitated and her voice was rising. "I mean, I'm almost thirty. And every time I meet a guy I like, I act idiotic. All I really want is a guy I can talk to—you know, the way I can talk to you, Mrs. Simpson...."

As disconcerting as it was to hear himself continually referred to as "Mrs. Simpson," Jackson could merely nod once more. Just moments ago, these had been his exact thoughts.

Ellen pressed a hand to one of her delectable breasts. Her cheeks were turning bright scarlet and the pulse was starting to tick rapidly in her throat. "I mean, I know what I look like. And I want a man who can appreciate that and—"

"And any man could," Jackson quickly put in.

"But there's more to me than how I look, Mrs. Simpson." She raced on, her voice deepening and stretching toward a crescendo. "I want a husband. I mean, I want a sex life. I *deserve* to start having sex, right? No one could expect me to go on like this! I don't want to be a virgin! I didn't *ask* to be a virgin!''

The sudden absence of her booming voice left a deafening silence.

Feeling stunned, Jackson managed to mumble something vague about how he was sure she'd meet the right man someday.

Her head was bobbing up and down, the way it did when she got seriously agitated. ''Well, that's the problem right now. I think I finally have met the right guy, Mrs. Simpson.''

Jackson didn't know which he felt more—relief or envy for the man whom she wanted to become her first lover. ''Who's that, m'dear?'' he managed to ask shakily.

''Your son,'' she said. ''Wyatt.''

4

"Good parallel action," Ellen whispered, whipping the Land Rover into a parking spot at Bernadette's General Store in Miracle Mountain. Wyatt's driving lessons had sure paid off. So had his guided tour around her fence line. Ellen still intended to confront that scoundrel Jackson West, but he *had* sold her a pretty piece of property, with lush timbered hillsides and a pond. Wyatt—who was so sweet, the complete opposite of what she imagined Jackson West would be like—had set up a bird feeder and a porch swing, from which Ellen had spotted a real live deer.

As for her contract—she'd promised she'd sign. For now that seemed enough. Abel's new songs wouldn't be ready to record for another month, and he'd agreed to cancel the Trash Cans' pending stage engagements. Ellen just wished she could come to some decisions about her future.

Right now, her whole life seemed like a "before and after" picture. Before Jean and Wyatt Simpson she'd used her ice princess persona and tough hysterical front to keep people at a distance. Now she was opening up in ways she never had. For so many years, while her father was drinking, she'd been afraid to let people in. Later, when she was singing, so many people seemed jealous. Or they wanted something. All the men ever seemed to want was sex. But then, all men weren't like that. Wyatt was interested in *her*. And because he had steadfastly ignored her temperamental outbursts—almost as if he knew how nervous he made her—Ellen now felt comfortable with him.

She stared through the plate-glass window of the general store, which was full of crafts and sundries, as well as barrels of bulk goods, dishes, bolts of brightly colored fabrics and handmade quilts. A few women milled around inside, and the place looked so homey that her heart suddenly ached. *Just remember what Mrs. Simpson said. You need to get out more.*

Maybe not, she thought moments later. When the string of bells attached to the doorknob quit ringing, the place was dead quiet. And everyone was staring at her. Ellen hazarded a quick glance down at her outfit—black opaque tights under cutoffs, pink combat boots, a lime green suede top she'd thought of as subdued only an hour ago, and a black leather jacket. Swallowing hard, she forced herself to remove her prescription sunglasses, letting them dangle around her neck by the leash. She wished she hadn't worn quite so many necklaces.

When the whispering started, most of it came from three well-dressed women huddled in a corner near the fabrics. Ellen guessed they were as close to the Junior League as it got in Miracle Mountain, Montana. The heaviest of the women had artfully streaked blond hair, pulled back with a giant plaid bow that matched her skirt. There was a thinner blonde in a bright red sweater set, and a woman with an auburn bob, who was wearing a navy pantsuit. All three gaped at Ellen's pink combat boots. She stared right back at their black pumps with the bows on the toes.

Just remember what Mrs. Simpson says. They're no better than you are. But being sized up by such women took Ellen back to the years after her mother died,

when well-intentioned community women kept visiting
to see if Ellen was being mistreated. She'd felt so sin-
gled out, embarrassed and angry. All she'd wanted was
to be left alone. Which was why she'd waited tables,
saved money—and fled to New York and L.A.

Yes, just standing in the store brought all the memories flooding back. The gossip. Feeling like a misfit.
How she always seemed to wear the wrong thing or
say something inappropriate. Ellen sighed. If Abel
hadn't coaxed her onto a stage, heaven only knew what
would have become of her.

Just do your shopping and ignore them. But the
looks made her nervous. Even though she tried to mod-
ulate her voice, she wound up bellowing at a sweet-
looking, gray-haired, bespectacled lady behind the cash
register. "Excuse me—" Ellen pulled an index card
from her back pocket "—but could you please direct
me to your fruit relish?"

"Right there, dear." The gray-haired lady pointed.

The woman was dressed in jeans and a wool sweater,
and she was probably in her fifties. Even from here,
Ellen could tell she had twinkling blue eyes behind her
glasses. Compared to the Junior Leaguers, she looked
really nice.

"Thanks." Ellen headed down the aisle, wishing her
combat boots didn't have metal taps. New York was
so noisy that she'd never noticed how much she jingled
and clanked when she walked. She blew out a short
sigh. *Face it. You've had a tough life. You're just not
the girl-next-door type. But that doesn't mean you're
not a good person. That's what Mrs. Simpson would
say.*

Fortunately, Ellen easily found the fruit relish, also
the spices and vanilla extract on her list. When she
turned toward the cash register again, she caught one

of the perky blond members of the Donna Reed club actually pointing at her. Her temper flared. She fought the wild urge to shout, *Puh-lease. Doris Days of the world unite!*

Not that Ellen had anything against Doris Day. She loved her movies. Especially the ones with Rock Hudson. And Ellen actually watched reruns of "The Donna Reed Show." Unfortunately, she was usually looking for pointers in how to be more normal.

Biting back another sigh, she told herself things could have been worse. She could have worn her black lipstick. She raised her voice. "Excuse me again. Could you please tell me where to find brown sugar, chopped nuts and cornstarch?" Even as she spoke, she winced at her own vocal register. Some days, she thought she should carry earplugs to offer any strangers within earshot.

The gray-haired lady behind the cash register didn't seem to notice. She frowned at the Doris Days, then, circling the counter, she said, "Here, maybe I'd better help. I'm Bernadette. This is my store. And you must be Purity."

Ellen concentrated on lowering her voice to a reasonable level. *Just be nice. As Mrs. Simpson always says, you have to give people the benefit of the doubt.* "Well...my real name's Ellen Smith."

Bernadette smiled. "Really? Why, that's a lovely name. Just..."

"So ordinary?" Ellen's lips suddenly twitched. No doubt Mrs. Simpson would make a point of extending the olive branch. "And I'd just love to meet your friends," she continued, having no illusions about making friends.

Predictably, the women turned their backs and pretended to discuss selections of cloth. Ellen shrugged.

"Well," she said loudly, "maybe when everybody's done with their shopping, Bernadette."

Lowering her voice, Bernadette whispered, "They don't mean to be rude. We just don't see many strangers—"

"And I imagine I'm strange," Ellen said, not fighting her pique. "Even for a stranger."

"Yes, well…" Bernadette glanced apologetically at the index card. "If you'll show me your recipe, I'll make sure you have everything you need."

"Thanks." Ellen sighed guiltily, handing her the card.

Bernadette squinted. "Why, I'd know this anywhere. It's Marilla West's plum pudding recipe."

In a town this size, probably anyone with the name West was related to Jackson the shyster. Maybe Marilla was his wife. "Oh, no," Ellen said quickly. "This is Mrs. Simpson's recipe." Ellen had wanted to surprise Wyatt with his favorite dessert tonight, so Mrs. Simpson had gladly given her the ingredients for plum pudding. Of course, Mrs. Simpson had suggested Ellen try shopping in Silver Spoon, but—like a fool—Ellen had decided to come to town.

Bernadette was gaping at her. "Whose recipe?"

"Mrs. Simpson's."

A loud gasp sounded behind her. "Not Mrs. *Jean* Simpson's!"

Ellen whirled around to find the three Junior Leaguers had stealthily approached. No doubt they were the most respectable women in town—and mean as rattlesnakes. She managed a cool nod. "Yes. I happen to be personal friends with Mrs. Jean Simpson, and she was kind enough to give it to me."

"Have you all met…Ellen Smith?" Bernadette said. The three pairs of eyes drifted slowly over Ellen's clothes, then the women quickly shook their heads. They may as well have exclaimed, "Most certainly not!" One finally said, "We thought your name was Purity."

"That's just a stage name."

"And you play for...the Can-Cans?"

Another said, "I think it's the Cash Cans."

Don't let them goad you. Ellen mustered her grandest tone, as if she played daily at Carnegie Hall. "The Trash Cans."

That seemed to be a real conversation stopper.

"Oh," someone finally said, as if that explained everything.

Then Bernadette formally introduced Ellen to Marjorie Nelson, Christine Clay and Phyllis Lewis; they headed the garden club, welcoming committee and church choir respectively.

Ellen's first thought was that the welcoming committee wasn't making her feel very welcome. Her second was that she'd love to sing with a church choir. She almost inquired about joining, then imagined her combat boots peeking out from beneath a choir robe. No, they probably wouldn't want her attending their church. Besides, with her luck, they thought heavy metal music was inspired by the devil himself.

"That's Jean Simpson's recipe?" the larger of the two blondes, Marjorie, finally asked.

Ellen nodded, feeling as if she were on trial.

The three women and Bernadette exchanged suspicious glances.

"Mrs. *Jean* Simpson's?" Phyllis clarified nervously, tucking auburn hair behind an ear. "From up on Little Miracle Road?"

"Yeah." That was the name of their road. Ellen glanced around, hoping they'd take the hint and leave,

so she could finish shopping. She'd had about enough
of the olive branch for one day.

"But Mrs. Simpson's dead," said Marjorie.

Ellen's temper flared. What was this? Some kind of
a test? "No she isn't. She's my housekeeper. I see her
practically every day." Except, of course, when she
couldn't make it, due to her lingering flu.

All the women gasped. And then they started talking
a mile a minute, as if Ellen wasn't even there. She
knew it was a good opportunity to drift away from the
group, but she was so shocked by what she heard that
she stayed. Apparently, Mrs. Simpson hadn't been seen
in town for years, and it was generally assumed she
had died from alcoholism.

Ellen leaned forward. "Mrs. Simpson was an alcoholic?" she finally said. No wonder Mrs. Simpson had
tensed when Ellen mentioned her father and Abel.

Marjorie said, "Her son, Wyatt, is, too."

"Oh, that's not true!" Ellen declared hotly. "Wyatt
comes over every day. He got all my appliances running. And you must have seen him in the store, since
he's been buying my groceries."

Bernadette shook her head. "I can't remember the
last time I saw Wyatt. If he bought groceries, he must
have done so in Silver Spoon."

"Surely these are just ugly, vicious rumors," Ellen
continued stridently. Feeling determined to stand up for
her new friends, she launched into a speech about all
the Simpsons had done for her. The women were held
spellbound.

"The Simpsons chop wood, build fires, cook and
clean?" echoed the women.

Ellen nodded.

"Well," Marjorie said, "Jean used to sing in the
choir, didn't she, Phyllis? And she was active in the

garden club. But that was years ago, before the tragedy...."

Ellen's heart lurched. "Tragedy?"

The woman started chattering again. And Ellen felt sicker by the minute. Mrs. Simpson's husband Garrett was rumored to have had an affair with a woman in Silver Spoon, and the love triangle led to his tragic suicide. Then Mrs. Simpson disappeared, and it was said that both she and Wyatt took to heavy drinking.

"My word," Ellen murmured in shock.

The next thing she knew, Marjorie was gripping her forearm. "Isn't that the saddest story you ever heard in your life?"

Ellen peered at Marjorie, thinking maybe the woman wasn't so bad, after all. "It is," she agreed. "But I know for a fact that Wyatt and his mother don't drink." After what had happened to her father and Abel, Ellen knew how to recognize all the signs of a heavy drinker.

"Well, do you think they quit?" asked Phyllis.

"I guess," said Ellen. She was barely able to process all this new information. Or that she was actually conversing with these women. She just wished her new friends, the Simpsons, had trusted her enough to confide in her. They'd fallen on hard times and become outcasts in their own community. It was no wonder Mrs. Simpson was so kind and empathetic. And that Wyatt, with his tousled blond hair and dreamy cornflower blue eyes, was so sensitive for a man.

"They've suffered," Ellen finally managed. "But believe me, they're fine now. In fact, they're the nicest people I've ever met. Mrs. Simpson is...like the mother I never had while I was growing up. And..." Color flooded her cheeks. "Well, I guess you could say Wyatt and I are dating." Oh, he hadn't kissed her yet. But they had dinner together most nights now.

The woman were staring at her, appalled. "You're dating Wyatt?" Marjorie said. "Wyatt *Simpson?*"

Ellen felt a rush of temper. The Simpsons had been so kind to her. Could she help restore their reputations? "Look…" Glancing down, Ellen took in the six, bow-toed pumps that formed a semicircle around her combat boots. For Mrs. Simpson and Wyatt, she decided she could do anything—including try to bridge some social differences. "Why don't you all drop by sometime? I know Mrs. Simpson would love to see you."

"Drop by?" the women repeated uncertainly.

Ellen nodded. "Most of the media's gone, but if the sheriff's there, have him call on his cell phone. I'll tell him to let you through my gate. Mrs. Simpson usually comes in the morning."

As the three women moved off, Bernadette winked. "None of us are very intimidating, not once you get to know us."

"Maybe not." Ellen swallowed hard. "But what would I serve them, if they actually show up to visit me?"

Bernadette chuckled heartily. "Don't worry. I stock all their favorite tea cakes. And maybe I'll visit, too."

PULLING her fuzzy pink sweater tightly around herself to ward off the chill night air, Ellen leaned back in the porch swing and gazed up. "You swear you caught that trout, Wyatt?"

He chuckled, setting aside his dessert dish. "You swear you made this plum pudding?"

"Just for you," she assured him, glancing around. She'd upended an orange crate and arranged a full box of tapers on top. Now, a dozen flaming tongues of fire flickered red and gold in the breeze, casting long shad-

ows on the porch floor. The candlelight turned his skin
a burnished copper.

Gingerly she leaned against him, and the warm heat
of his hard body made her throat close, stealing her
breath. If only he'd take the hint and kiss her. So many
times now, they'd been this close.

Earlier tonight, as he'd shown her how to fillet the
trout he'd brought, he'd snuggled right behind her, his
arms around her waist, and his broad chest warming
her back as his huge hand, closed over hers, guided the
knife. While he took her through all the motions of
preparing the fish, he'd explained each step in a soft,
patient drawl that made her shiver with anticipation.

Now if only he would turn. And she would turn. And
then she'd tilt up her face while he angled his down....

He was so easy to talk to, unless the subject was
their relationship—if that's what this was. If he weren't
such a good Christian—just as his mother had
claimed—would he have hauled off and kissed her by
now? Should she make the first move? *But what if I'm
wrong and he's not even interested? Oh, just kiss him.
The worst thing that can happen is that he'll reject you.*

Ellen's heart hammered. What if they wound up in
bed immediately? There was that kind of chemistry between them—at least on her side. She'd even mustered
her nerve and bought condoms at Bernadette's. Which
meant everybody in town probably already knew she
had designs on Wyatt—except Wyatt.

Putting his arm around her, he drew her closer; his
jean jacket fell open and her cheek wound up pressed
against his shirt. Beneath the warm plaid flannel, she
could hear the steady beat of his heart.

"My, you sure look serious, sugar."

"I...heard some rumors in town today about your

family." Her eyes searched his, hoping to communicate that he could talk about his feelings with her.

He merely looked cautious. "My family?"

She nodded. "But I told everybody that things were different now," she said quickly. "I told them all you'd done for me around here...."

His expression was turning grim. She should have known he'd want to talk about his life in his own time. How could she have been so insensitive? "Sorry, Wyatt...." she murmured.

His arm tightened around her. "No, *I'm* sorry."

The testiness of his tone made her hate every bad thing that had ever befallen him. No doubt, he felt as prickly about his past as she did about hers. She rubbed a hand soothingly over his chest, wrinkling his flannel shirt, then smoothing it.

Something flickered in his eyes, as if there were a thousand things he wanted to say and he couldn't settle on just one. "Oh, El," he finally sighed.

She loved his nickname for her. "Hmm?"

He turned slowly toward her, raised a hand and brushed his thumb lightly across her cheek. "Look, I'm...I'm not the man you think I am." His lips were compressed in a tight line. Clearly he wanted to go on, but he simply couldn't. It always seemed so difficult for men to talk about their feelings. She decided it was probably even worse for cowboys.

"I didn't mean to pry," she said.

"You're not prying."

Cradling her hand in his, he curled it against his chest. Then his dusty boot heels pushed them off, and they swung for a few minutes in silence. She became conscious of how the chill air was making her cheeks tingle, and of the night sounds from the hills—leaves rustling in the wind, wings fluttering as birds took flight, the whir of crickets and the hoot of an owl. Finally she said, "Well, did you guys finally get the rest of the cows down?"

At the mention of ranch work, he looked relieved. "Yeah, but I found some of Logan Hatcher's cattle mixed in with the Herefords. I can't believe roundup's already over. By January, I'll be awake all night, between the calving and the branding."

"I hope it's not as cold as last winter." He'd already told her countless stories about how the previous harsh winter had affected the herd.

"Me, too. I swear, last year it was everything we could do to keep those cows warm. Shoot, me and the boys even took some sick calves inside the house. A bunch lost their ears and tails to frostbite...."

Ellen smiled, loving the faraway look he got in his eyes when he talked about ranching. Jackson West apparently owned a large herd, and Wyatt could talk a full hour about one specific cow. He was a born cowboy, and she wished he didn't have to work for Jackson. He deserved his own ranch.

"Ellen, you don't really want to hear about a bunch of old cows."

She smiled. "Are you kidding? I love it when you talk about brush hogging and the perils of larkspur poisoning."

When he chuckled, the corners of his eyes crinkled, and the candlelight brought out the blue fire of his eyes. "That's how I talk sexy."

Ellen, he wouldn't say something like that if he didn't feel some attraction to you. And he wouldn't cuddle with you on the porch swing, either. But she had trouble trusting her emotions. And a lifetime with her unpredictable father had made her skittish when it came to reading other people's behavior. She edged closer. "Ever dream of having your own ranch?"

He merely squinted, as if wondering what she was talking about, then awareness flooded his eyes. "Uh...sure." Instead of elaborating, he quickly contin- ued. "C'mon, cows can't be nearly as interesting as playing in a band. I bought your records, you know."

Her eyes widened. "You listened to them?"

He nodded. "I liked the couple of slow songs the best. I could hear you sing better."

She smiled ruefully. He meant songs such as "Bal- lad of a Bad Man." Songs in which her voice had to work, circling flat notes, stretching for high ones. Those songs were the reason she practiced scales for hours every day. She sighed wistfully. "I wish Abel would write more ballads. If I was a songwriter, I would."

"But you were writing songs in the bedroom that day...."

Her cheeks, so cool from the night air, warmed with inner heat. She laughed. "I lied. I...was embarrassed and shy around you, and I didn't want you to know I was just hiding out in the bedroom whenever you came over. I never wrote a song in my life. And before you tell me I should try, please take my word for it. I don't have the talent."

He frowned. "Could you record songs for somebody else?"

"I don't know. Most people record their own songs. I guess I could do commercials, but I'd be taking a step backward."

"Not if that's what you want to do."

It was so like something his mother would say. She shrugged. "I like heavy metal. But I hate the clubs." Pain suddenly twisted inside her, and she tried to find the words to explain. "I mean, I *really* hate them. I hate the smoke, the smell of booze, all those loud people." Her throat constricted with emotion. "I guess it's...always reminded me of my dad. Before he died, I used to have to track him down in bars. He drank in dives, too, and they were always smoky, full of leering guys. I guess that's why I don't drink at all. And maybe it's why, unless I'm singing, I get nervous when men look at me...."

His voice was heartbreakingly tender. "Does my looking at you make you nervous, El?"

A little. "At first. Not now." She sighed. "Funny, that I wound up singing in bars...."

His voice was tender. "You think it's 'cause they were familiar to you, sugar?"

She relaxed, feeling the soft rocking of the swing. "Maybe. But it's more like, by throwing myself into that environment, I get the illusion I can control it. It's just an act, a performance, and with everybody watching, I'm in control...."

"I think I understand."

Her eyes searched his. "I know this sounds weird, but when I sing on stage, I feel as if none of the bad things ever happened—as if my mother's still alive. And my father never started drinking. But I do know it's only an illusion."

"Maybe that's why you're not rarin' to sign that new contract. Maybe you're changing. Maybe you don't need illusions anymore."

He was so perceptive. It was funny how that was often true of people who'd suffered the most. People with tragic lives were usually the quickest to laugh, too. "I guess being in the general store today made me think about all this stuff, because the women intimidated me. Maybe I didn't turn out to be the plaid skirt and navy blazer type, but I tried to do the best I could for myself, given what I had."

He slowly stroked her hair. "Sugar, you turned out to be as close to perfection as it gets."

Her voice caught with emotion. "Thanks."

"I mean it."

"Uh…" She traced a nonsensical pattern on his shirt with her fingernail. "You know, we've had a lot of fun lately."

He nodded, as if wondering where she was heading. "Yeah."

Licking at her lips, she forged ahead. "Well, don't take this wrong, but I've never been around a guy so long who didn't try to kiss me. I don't mean to embarrass you, but aren't you…even the least little bit attracted to me?"

He looked stunned. "Of course."

She swallowed nervously. "And is my personality okay?"

His lips twisted in a thoroughly bemused smile. "El, I love hanging out here. Swinging and talking until late at night.…"

"But you'd just like to be friends? Is that it?"

She wasn't really sure, but she thought he looked faintly uncomfortable. "Well, friendship's important. And I never really was good friends with a woman. I mean, I've been trying to be friends."

"So, you're not interested in…*more.*"

Warring emotions crossed his face. His lips parted, as if he might say something, then compressed into another thin line. "You…don't really know me."

So that was it. He wanted to tell her about his life, but he wasn't ready. Her throat felt so dry now that she could barely talk. "Wyatt, I…I know you as well as I need to." *To kiss you.*

He seemed to know exactly what she meant. And he shook his head firmly. "No, you don't."

"Well, then, tell me whatever I need to know."

He stared at her for a long moment. "Believe me, if you found out about me, you'd run me off your property with that rifle in there." He loosed a low whistle. "In fact, now that I've taught you to shoot, I figure I might wind up with a bullet in my backside, sugar."

Her lips quirked. He was so sweet. "I think that's a bit dramatic, Wyatt. This is me. Purity. Lead singer of the Trash Cans. Whatever it is, I think I can handle it."

He shook his head again.

Well, he'd admitted to liking her looks and personality. So she'd just have to take the bull by the horns and get aggressive with this cowboy. She pressed herself against his side, slid her palm around the back of his neck and lowered her voice so that it came out breathless and throaty. "Wyatt, is it because you're a Christian? I mean, even really good Christians kiss, you know. Even Billy Graham. Have you ever thought about kissing me?"

He was starting to look stricken. "Uh...yeah."

Her pride was definitely taking a back seat to her heartfelt attraction to this man. She gazed soulfully into his eyes. "So why don't you? I swear I won't bite."

"El, this just...just isn't right."

"Please."

He swallowed so hard she heard it. Looking faintly embarrassed, he said, "Making our relationship physical is a big step. I want you to think about it."

She wasn't backing down. "It's all I *ever* think about."

Looking more worried, he edged away—until he seemed to realize she had him trapped in the corner of the porch swing. *It's just rejection,* she thought. *No big deal. You'll live.* "I thought you said you liked me."

"I do." His eyes cast around, as if desperately searching for the words to best explain his feelings. He finally settled on, "Sugar, I think you're the best thing since sliced bread."

Not exactly eloquent, but it would certainly do. Still, if it was true, he'd kiss her. Which meant he probably just didn't want to hurt her feelings. "It's okay. I understand."

He gave a frustrated sigh. "No, you don't."

"Yes I do. And it's fine."

"It is *not* fine."

"Enough said. Just drop it." Edging away from his chest, she felt hot color sting her cheeks as she turned to face him. Her voice started to rise. "Please. Let's just forget everything I've said tonight. In fact, I can't believe I bared my soul this way. How humiliating. I don't know what came over me. I'm so sorry. You're probably just putting your arm around me to be nice—"

"To be nice?" he gasped.

Muttering a sudden oath, he abruptly hauled her against the hard muscles of his chest as his mouth crushed down on hers. The warm, honeyed spear of his tongue followed, swift and sure. And as it delved deep, making slow heat start to dance in her veins, Ellen could merely cling to his neck, shuddering against him.

She'd known it would be good, but nothing like this. Never like this. The urgency of his mouth made her whole body burn for him—made her breasts feel full and heavy, aching for the touch of his hands. She might not have much experience. But she'd been wrong to assume he didn't want her. That much she knew now. His kiss was proof he'd just been holding back.

When he drew away, his lips still hovering, she could merely stare. "You kiss like you've had some experience," she murmured raspily.

Between nips at her lips, he whispered, "You thought I hadn't?"

"Well, the way your mother talked, I just assumed..."

"Mothers," he responded huskily, right before his hot hungry lips claimed hers again, "don't always know everything about their sons."

5

THE ABSENCE OF NECKLACES and boots made Ellen unusually quiet as she paced around the living room. Her platinum hair was neatly gathered into a fluffy ponytail, and Jackson decided the conservative, new, red-and-navy plaid bow that held it back didn't suit her nearly as much as the rest of her outfit—a black turtleneck and oversize jeans, held up by skinny purple suspenders. The gold horseshoe pin skewered to a suspender wasn't really her style, either.

Whirling on the heel of a high-top sneaker, Ellen began adding logs to the fire in the wood-burning stove. "Are you sure I didn't do anything wrong, Mrs. Simpson?"

"Of course not, m'dear," Jackson said, smoothing his dress. "But your house is just about in apple-pie order, now, isn't it?"

"I guess. But you keep trying to quit, so I feel as if I've...done something."

"Of course not."

Except you kissed me, El. And you think my name is really Wyatt Simpson. Or Jean Simpson. Now Jackson couldn't let this charade go on a second longer. He'd been awake half the night, battling his desire and his conscience. Not to mention reliving every touch of her untutored lips. Oh, Ellen had started it. But he'd finished it. He'd tried to make it short and sweet. But his tender kisses had caught fire as fast as dry kindling, engendering a blistering heat that had lasted longer than a month of summer Sundays.

He hadn't kissed anybody like that in years—if ever. Hell, after a man reached a certain age, women were more likely to invite him to bed than to a candlelit porch swing under the moon and stars. Jackson didn't know if it was the novelty of a little romance, or of kissing a woman with whom he was friends—but last night, he'd wound up hauling El right onto his lap and making out with her until long after midnight, like some randy teen. And even though he'd had no intention of taking advantage of the situation and sleeping with her, he'd let himself get all hot and bothered anyway. By the time he'd herded himself back to the ranch, he'd felt crazy as a loon—downright out of his mind—from wanting her. It hadn't helped to hear her coo what she thought was his name against his cheeks. "Wyatt," she'd sighed over and over. "Oh, Wyatt."

Don't start torturing yourself again, Jackson. But it was too late. Already, heat had pooled low in his belly at the memories. Swift, insistent pangs tugged at both his body and heart, and something that felt like sawdust hit the back of his throat. He might be traipsing around her house today, wearing a dress like a darn woman, but every time Jackson looked at her, he was reminded that his pink jumper hid a hundred-percent hard, uncompromising male.

He stared at her now, recalling the way she'd looked last night—her well-kissed mouth slack, her velvet brown eyes glazed. Because of their deepening friendship, she'd been so open to him, so vulnerable. There was no pretense, no coyness. And now Jackson wanted to go back in time and relive that moment when, in her husky voice, she'd whispered, "Please take me to bed, Wyatt."

He almost had. He didn't even care that she didn't know he was Jackson West. He'd never wanted to make love to a woman so badly. He still wanted Logan's property, too. But if Ellen ever found out she'd been used, it would destroy her. No, he'd rather break his own heart now—and end it. Besides, the woman had torn him up inside more than tangled barbed wire ever could.

Last night she'd scared him. He could admit that now. She'd cast those wanton sheep's eyes in his direction and brought out the predatory wolf. And yet, he thought, glancing down at the jumper, he was really a wolf in sheep's clothing. And she deserved better.

Besides, he definitely wanted more than sex. Playing this charade had let him know El as he'd never known another woman. He was falling hard for her mix of city sophistication, offbeat charm, and down-home innocence. She made him long for shared meals and couch cuddling. Because beneath her flair for drama and her prickly defensiveness, Jackson had discovered what no man ever had—her desperate need to be loved. And that need was bringing him to his knees.

Which was why he had to resign as Mrs. Simpson. If—while he was pretending to be Wyatt—El asked him again to make love, they'd both be goners. He'd lift her in his arms, carry her to the nearest bed and slowly, deftly initiate her. He wanted to leave his mark, to claim and possess and teach her everything he knew. All night, alone in his bed, he'd ached for it. He'd imagined the touch of her long slender fingers and fantasized about becoming the first man to be thoroughly explored by them.

"Mrs. Simpson?"

Jackson blinked.

"Whatever you're thinking, you can just tell me."

Hardly.

"Not a thing, m'dear." Jackson busied himself by straightening the jars of creams on the table. "Now, Ellen," he ventured again in a high-pitched falsetto, "you're not the only person in town who needs a housekeeper, you know." As El crossed the room and leaned against a window frame, he glanced at her over his shoulder.

Ellen merely scowled. "And don't look at me like that."

Even though his throat was starting to ache from speaking at such a high pitch, he raised his voice again. "Like what?"

"Like I'm personally responsible for every dust bunny between here and Silver Spoon."

Jackson sighed. "Well, I do have other clients." At least he hoped she'd believe it and let him go.

Ellen frowned grumpily. Even in the morning light, her brown eyes looked as softly luminous as a moonlit midnight sky. Just looking at her, Jackson felt wistful.

"Darla didn't warn me there was a limit to the length of time you could work," she protested. "Besides, now I...I think of you as my friend."

Friends. Jackson guessed they'd become that, no matter how strange the circumstances. He didn't want this friendship destroyed, either. He *had* to get out of here. Oh, he told himself it was because he could now put on lipstick in the pitch dark and not miss his lip line. Shoot, even Darla agreed this wasn't funny anymore. If it ever had been. But the real reason he had to leave was because he couldn't risk hurting El.

Ellen suddenly gasped. "Oh, no. They came."

Jackson's heart hammered. "They who?"

When El didn't bother to answer, he moved next to her at the window. His eyes widened. An army of women was charging up the hill. He knew every darn one of them, too. The three nibbiest biddies in town—Marjorie Nelson, Christine Clay and Phyllis Lewis—led the way. Bernadette was behind them with Jackson's own great-aunt Sarah, who was hanging on to her cane with one hand and Bernadette with the other.

Jackson turned and headed straight for the back door, but Ellen grabbed his arm and held fast. She spoke in a breathless rush. "Please don't be mad. Oh, Mrs. Simpson, I know I should have told you. But when I was in town yesterday, I heard all about your troubles—about your husband's affair and suicide and about how you and Wyatt started drinking and…" She paused long enough to gulp down a breath. "And I— I told them how different everything is now. That you're the nicest woman I know. And that I'm dating Wyatt—"

"Dating Wyatt!" Jackson bet those women were having a field day with that information. He thought of the real Wyatt—with his scraggly black hair and surly temper, locked up in the alcoholism ward of the hospital. He gaped at Ellen, horrified.

"Please don't be mad! I just can't help but like Wyatt. Any woman would. And he even kissed me last night. Do you mind? Do you *really* mind?"

Jackson's head was spinning. Now, he forgot about Wyatt—and remembered El's lips against his own. "Uh…no."

"So it's okay if your son and I are pursuing a…"

Physical relationship. The unspoken words hung in the air, and El was peering up at him, her earnest eyes begging for his approval.

"I'm, uh, very pleased, m'dear." That was an understatement. Jackson would like nothing more than a physical relationship—as soon as he was no longer spending his mornings in a dress. And his evening pretending to be Wyatt Simpson.

"I am *very* serious about Wyatt," Ellen stressed.

As if he'd think *she* was using *him*. Jackson sighed. Fortunately, there wasn't more time to contemplate the fact that, at this rate, he could become his own mother-in-law.

Ellen rushed on. "Well, anyway, I figured if you suspected the church ladies were coming that you might want to run…"

Run wasn't the word.

Jackson started for the back door again. But she maintained her grip on him. He really couldn't believe this. The only reason he'd donned this damnable dress today was so he could quit the housekeeping job. Now his heart was beating dangerously hard, and his great-aunt Sarah and her cronies were getting closer by the second. Ellen looked as stricken as he felt.

"I don't have any chairs," she said in a panic.

"Chairs?" The woman was thinking about chairs at a time like this?

"And napkins," she said. "Oh, no. I forgot napkins."

"That's the least of our troubles." Yanking away his arm, Jackson beelined for the back door. He hadn't moved this fast since junior high, when Polly Pearl's papa had chased him out of their hayloft with a shotgun. El scurried after him. This time, she snatched his clothes, then stuck to his back like a wet T-shirt. How in thunder could she have put him in this position?

Feeling livid, Jackson spun around. Ellen lost her grip on the tentlike pink jumper and staggered backward. Suddenly the significance of El's gold horseshoe pin and plaid hair bow hit him and his heart ached for her. She'd bought new, conservative accessories hoping to impress these women.

At the realization, he had to fight not to pull her into his arms and rain kisses all over her hair. El would probably fit into Miracle Mountain, Montana, society about as well as a lamb in a horse corral. But she was trying. Oh, she might fool herself into thinking this was all for Mrs. Simpson. But it was El who wanted to fit in—and she felt she never had, anywhere. Damn. Jackson wanted to take her right up to the ranch house, have his ma fix her a hot meal and then introduce her to his siblings, who would shower her with love. They'd appreciate how sweet she really was…. *Lordy, Jackson! Now's not the time to get philosophical about Ellen. Get moving!*

But her hand was wrapped icily around his arm. "Mrs. Simpson," she begged. "Please, don't blow it. I told them you don't drink. That you're…different now. That you didn't die or run off. And that Darla from the beauty salon swears you're the best available housekeeper. Please, don't let me down…."

Jackson uttered a soft curse.

"Excuse me?"

"Nothing, m'dear."

But against this crew, Jackson didn't stand a chance. The only saving grace was that his great-aunt Sarah was both visually- and hearing-impaired. He sighed. Drawing in a deep breath, he exhaled, and in his loftiest soprano said, "I guess we could bring in that old picnic bench from out back."

If he was wondering at his own motives, the answer came when El flung her arms around his neck, uttering a breathless "I absolutely *adore* you, Mrs. Simpson."

They set out to move the bench indoors, and just as they finished positioning it in front of the couch, the knock sounded. Jackson held his breath as El ushered in their guests. To his surprise, the women started hugging him, fussing over him, wringing his hands and telling him how wonderful he looked. No doubt they were just trying to be polite.

Marjorie finally said hesitantly, "Heavens, Jean, all this time we thought you were...dead."

It was a rather awkward thing to say. But at least no one had shrieked, "It's Jackson West!"

Within minutes, Jackson was passing the bite-size tea cakes while El poured tea in dainty china cups she said she'd bought at Bernadette's. After everyone was served, he and Ellen sat on the couch and stared at the five women. The women seated on the picnic bench awkwardly balanced dainty saucers on their knees and stared back.

Finally Marjorie spoke, "I was just telling Phyllis how good it is to see you, Jean. Wasn't I, Phyllis?"

Phyllis nodded. "Jean, you look...quite a bit different."

Now there's *an understatement,* Jackson thought.

Bernadette quickly said, "But Phyllis doesn't mean that in a bad way, Jean."

I'll bet. Jackson knew he wasn't going to win any beauty contests. "It's insides not outsides that count," he couldn't help but remind them.

A long silence fell.

If they were waiting for an explanation of Mrs. Simpson's sudden reappearance in town, they weren't going to get it. Crossing his feet in what he hoped was a ladylike fashion, Jackson glanced down to where his saucer and cup were balanced on his palm. Suddenly his callused hands seemed huge, almost brutish against the dainty cup. Ellen nervously squeezed his arm, to reassure him or herself—he wasn't sure which. In the ever-stretching silence, cups clinked against saucers, and Ellen's eyes darted around, as if she couldn't think of anything to say.

Jackson looked at her anxious face and felt his heart breaking. She was so desperate for this visit to be a success. Well, if there was one thing he knew, it was how to start female tongues wagging. Using bits and pieces from his mother's phone conversations and praying his voice wouldn't crack, he said, "I've been out of circulation for so long! So, what's happening? How's the store, Bernie? And Mr. Canning's hardware? And Mary Louise Landers—why, I heard she's left the church choir in a huff...."

At the mention of Mary Louise, the room exploded with gossip. By degrees, El's death grip relaxed. Of course, Jackson should have known the conversation would eventually circle around to Dusty's bar. And he didn't want to think about Dusty right now.

When Jackson had remembered to take out the bag of El's old clothes, he'd been dressed in jeans. He'd run right into Dusty, who'd merrily tossed the clothes into his pickup, mistakenly thinking Jackson was fulfilling phase two of the bet with Logan. Now the moose at Dusty's bar was wearing one of El's corsets.

Jackson smoothed his pink skirt in his lap, then he watched Phyllis nervously tuck a lock of her auburn bob behind her ear. "Dusty plays that jukebox until all hours of the night!" she said.

Marjorie reached behind her, tightening a plaid bow in her hair that was identical to El's. "Well, you know they play high-stakes poker in Dusty's backroom."

"Strip poker, I heard," Christine added.

"Well, whatever it is," Phyllis said, "it's gambling."

Jackson's great-aunt Sarah shook her head, scandalized. "No doubt, my nephew Jackson is in the thick of it."

Jackson's lips parted in protest. Most of what they were saying wasn't true. Dusty didn't even have a backroom. And now El was going to get an even worse impression of him. He suddenly realized he had vague plans about coming clean, introducing himself as Jackson West, and then dating Ellen. *Not in this lifetime,* he thought. Nevertheless—and in spite of the risk—he cleared his throat and spoke again. "But I remember Jackson as being such a nice young man...."

Christine gasped. "Jean, that man's thirty-three years old and he hasn't even thought of settling down!"

Jackson felt a rush of temper. He thought about marrying and having a family all the time. Besides, what would Christine Clay know about him—or his life?

"He dates them and drops them," announced Phyllis.

"Well, he *is* sinfully good-looking," said Christine.

"True," Jackson couldn't help but put in.

Ellen's head was starting to bob, the way it did when she was particularly annoyed. "You know, he sold me this shack for a half a million dollars."

Everybody looked positively stunned.

"Here, wait." Ellen hopped up, ran for the bedroom and returned with the tiny square ad she'd kept from the *Los Angeles Times*. Carefully unfolding it, she passed it around. One by one, the women read it.

"I always liked Jackson," Bernadette finally said with a sigh. "I'm shocked he'd engage in real-estate fraud."

His great-aunt Sarah crossed her arms angrily. "My niece Marilla's going to hear about this. Honey, we'll get your money back. Even with fifty good acres, that's hardly a fair price.''

Ellen sighed. ''To tell you the truth, I've had such a hard time learning to trust men....''

Marjorie shook her head. ''And then a *man* goes and does something like this!'' Marjorie spit out the word *man* as if it were a curse.

Ellen impulsively squeezed Jackson's arm. ''Of course, Mrs. Simpson's son, Wyatt, has really helped me. I just wish he owned his own ranch, instead of having to work for Jackson.'' She glanced away from the guests. ''I'm sorry, Mrs. Simpson, but Wyatt's so sweet. I don't think Jackson pays him nearly enough. He obviously loves ranching and he works so hard....''

''I guess you really *are* dating him,'' said Marjorie.

Bernadette tittered. ''The girl's half in love, if you ask me.''

''Has he kissed you?'' asked Marjorie.

Color flooded El's cheeks. ''For the first time last night,'' she admitted, her eyes dreamy. ''And he's the best kisser.''

All the women leaned eagerly forward.

Great-aunt Sarah didn't look at all convinced that this was good. ''Who cares about kissing?'' she demanded. ''Is he a gentleman? That's the important thing.''

''I practically had to *force* him to kiss me,'' said Ellen.

''Good,'' said great-aunt Sarah with an approving nod.

''Well,'' Marjorie said, ''from what I remember of your son, Jean Simpson, he *was* circumspect when it came to women.'' She glanced at El. ''You can bet a man like Wyatt hasn't been around the block a million times.''

"Unlike my nephew," put in Jackson's great-aunt.

Jackson had heard enough. He'd had no idea his reputation was this bad. And to have his own great-aunt Sarah malign him. Sure, he dated regularly, but he hardly bedded down with every woman he took out to supper. He fought the urge to stand up, rip off his wig, expose himself as Jackson West and tell them all where to go. He would have, but he knew how much this visit meant to Ellen. So he just sat there in his vile Mrs. Simpson costume and fumed.

"Well," El was saying, "I guess you can't compare a man like Wyatt to a man like Jackson West."

As she launched into a heartfelt monologue about all the things Wyatt had done to make her house habitable, jealousy ripped through Jackson. It was he, not Wyatt, who'd done all those things for her. Wyatt—the real Wyatt—was a no-account drunk. Even now, Jackson was trying to get Wyatt sober—and at his own personal expense since Wyatt didn't have insurance. He sighed in frustration, just wishing El knew what he was going through. Sitting here on pins and needles, feeling as if he might be exposed any minute. And all for her sake. When she was done singing Wyatt's praises, Jackson cleared his throat. "Now, I'm sure Jackson has tried to help Wyatt...."

All the women whirled on him, looking rabid.

"Oh, Jean," reprimanded Phyllis. "It's good of you to want to turn the other cheek—it *is* the Christian thing—but from what Ellen says, Jackson is taking advantage of poor Wyatt and working him half to death."

"Mrs. Simpson is always so sweet," Ellen added. "*Too* sweet."

"Before all your troubles," declared Marjorie, "you always were a saint, Jean."

Jackson couldn't believe it. Because of his feeble

attempt to defend himself, they were turning Mrs. Simpson into a martyr, when Mrs. Simpson—the real Mrs. Simpson—was dead. At least so far as Jackson knew.

I'm the one who's a saint, he thought angrily. Under the table, he'd done countless charitable acts. And when his own father died, Jackson had wordlessly taken over the Bar Triple Cross—even though it meant he'd never go to college and study agriculture, the way he'd always wanted....

Thankfully the conversation had turned to minister Martin. All the women were convinced that the lonely widower needed a new love interest. Jackson was relieved until Phyllis suddenly enthused, "What about you, Jean?"

Jackson choked on his tea cake. Surely he'd misunderstood. He rapidly shook his head.

"Oh, you two could at least go to dinner," chided Marjorie.

As the discussion of his romantic prospects with minister Martin heated up, Jackson's mind raced. Lordy, this had gone way too far! He had to find a way out of this mess—right now. He was so deep in thought, that he barely noticed when the visitors started rising; goodbye chatter swirled around him.

"Well, Jean, it was so wonderful to see you," said Marjorie. "And the tea cakes were lovely, Ellen. My favorite."

"You're such a sweet girl," said Phyllis. "Nothing like it says in those magazines. And, Jean, I can't wait to see you again."

Ellen beamed. "Thank you all so much for coming."

Pausing at the door, Jackson's great-aunt Sarah smiled. "You'll definitely be there, then?"

Jackson had no idea what had transpired while he was ruminating about his miserable situation. Not that it mattered. Great-aunt Sarah didn't wait for a response. Instead, she glanced around with a final sigh of satisfaction.

"These changes in you are so commendable, Jean. An inspiration for the entire community. So we're pleased you and Wyatt have decided to come to church on Sunday with Ellen."

Jackson shook his head. "But I—"

"We'll see you there!" said Ellen.

JACKSON LEANED BACK in his swivel chair at the ranch office, the phone tucked between his jaw and shoulder. "There's no way I can make it on Sunday, El."

"But your mother and I told everybody you'd come."

"I...have to work."

"Hmm. Well I wish you could. And that your mom was here."

His heart pulled. El was at her place, all alone. And he wanted nothing more than to be there—massaging her hands, brushing her hair, painting her toenails. He sighed at the memories, then felt a twinge of sadness. Right now, El was hiding out. But she was talented. She'd sign her contract or find other work. She wouldn't be here forever. "Lonesome?"

"Yeah. But I thought I might go hiking...."

"Dress warm," he said. "It's nippy."

"You sound just like your mother."

"Hmm." He sighed, listening to her throaty voice as she talked about her plans for the day. At least she believed that Wyatt had to work at the ranch on Sunday. Now if Jackson could only invent an excuse for Mrs. Simpson. It was too bad Jackson couldn't be himself—dust off his one good suit and escort Ellen to church.

He guessed he should clean out Wyatt's cabin soon, since he was determined to end the Mrs. Simpson charade. He'd left the ironing board set up, and makeup and wigs on the dresser. Should he simply vanish? Just clean the cabin and throw away all Mrs. Simpson's clothes? Wyatt would get out of rehab and the strange reappearance of Mrs. Simpson would remain a mystery forever. Trouble was, that plan meant giving up Ellen. Besides, Ellen would send out a search party if Mrs. Simpson disappeared.

"Well," she finally said, "I guess I'd better let you go before Jackson yells at you for being on the ranch phone."

There it was again. The assumption that Jackson West was an ogre. "Jackson won't mind. You know, he's *really* not a bad guy...."

She sighed. "I wish you didn't always defend him."

"Let's talk about something else, El."

"Like what?"

He chuckled softly. "Like what you're wearing."

There was a long pause. Then she breathlessly began, "It's skimpy and lacy...."

Listening to her fairly innocent teasing, Jackson bit back a moan. Since their first kiss, he'd kissed her every chance he got. With every touch of her lips, he wound up wanting to carry her over the threshold of the doorway to oblivion. He sighed, feeling sure he couldn't live without her.

"Wyatt?"

For a second, he forgot he was supposed to answer to that name. "Hmm?"

"I think I'm falling for you," she suddenly said.

And Jackson had never felt more exhilarated—or more trapped by his own gambling nature.

As THE SONOROUS CHORDS of the organ faded and minister Martin launched into his sermon, El whispered, "I can't believe Jackson made Wyatt work on a Sunday when he wanted so badly to come to church."

And Jackson really couldn't believe he was sitting in a church pew dressed in Mrs. Simpson's best navy suit. At least the suit had a matching, wide-brimmed hat which, along with the gray wig and glasses, obscured nearly every inch of Jackson's face.

Still, he was beginning to think this wasn't a church at all, but some heaven-sent punishment he sorely deserved. He could admit it. He'd led a life of vice—of gambling, roughhousing and drinking with the boys. But all week he'd tried to wheedle his way out of paying for his sins in this excruciating way—only to find he was powerless to deny Ellen anything.

"Working on a Sunday," El fumed. "After the service, I'm going to Jackson West's ranch and chew him out. I haven't even confronted him about the property I bought—yet."

Jackson wanted to say that cows needed care twenty-four hours a day, Sundays included. And that he paid doubletime; the cowboys on the ranch wanted to work. Instead he murmured, "The sermon, m'dear."

Maybe it would inspire El to turn the other cheek. As much as she stewed about Jackson, he was surprised she hadn't turned up at the ranch already. But it was inevitable. When she did, he had no idea how he'd handle it.

He concentrated on the minister's smooth baritone, which projected over polished wood pews filled with people Jackson recognized. Crystal and Austin. His mother. His sister, Darla, who was seated across the aisle, next to his great-aunt Sarah. On the way inside, Darla had sidled close and teased, "So this is what it takes to get a sinner like you to church."

It was true Jackson hadn't come to church in years. And it wasn't so bad. A glorious autumn sunlight streamed in through the stained-glass windows, casting hints of colored light on the tile floor. Up front, urns of white flowers sat on linen-covered altar tables. He'd forgotten how peaceful it was.

Jackson hadn't prayed for years, either—not since his father was sick, and then, not formally. But he decided he could definitely use some help of a divine order right about now. Somehow, this foolhardy, crazy charade had to end—and without El getting hurt. His eyes drifted toward her. She was wearing a simple knit knee-length black dress and high heels. She sure was gorgeous. He might be in the Church of the Lamb, wearing Mrs. Simpson's suit, but he was still the most hot-blooded man he knew.

Not that he cared about that. *Just keep her from getting hurt,* Jackson suddenly thought. Maybe it was a prayer. He wasn't sure.

Then minister Martin intoned, "Mrs. Simpson."

Jackson nearly leapt out of his seat. Was minister Martin preaching about Wyatt and his mother? His eyes shot to El. She smiled back, a soft sweet smile that curved the corner of her mouth near her mole. Reaching for his hand, she gave it a quick squeeze.

Minister Martin's baritone continued, "As we all know, after Garrett Simpson's tragic suicide, further misfortune befell Brother Wyatt, who unfortunately couldn't be here today, and Sister Jean, who was long thought dead. But Sister Jean Simpson is truly reborn and among the living now. And she and her son, by transforming themselves, have given us all cause to rejoice. Let them be symbols for our little community in Miracle Mountain.

"Yes, folks—" his voice now rose thunderously "—there's been a little miracle on Little Miracle Road. A case of everyday redemption. How I wish all people could reach out as Ellen Smith has in our community. Her other name, Purity, is well deserved. A stranger in our midst, she's brought our own lost brethren back into the fold. She's proved that bridges can be built—between the rich and poor, the old and young, the high and low."

Jackson wanted to die. Every eye in the place was misting up. Darla looked as guilty as he felt. The real Mrs. Simpson, as far as Jackson knew, was deader than a doornail. And Wyatt was still in the hospital and none too thrilled about his newfound sobriety.

"God works in some very mysterious ways," intoned the minister.

"He sure does," whispered Jackson.

"So, let us make our bridges strong." Minister Martin's voice rose to a crescendo. "Can't we all get along?"

Jackson's eyes didn't sting—he hadn't even cried when his father died, but he did suddenly wish the world could be a better place. And that he could be a better person.

"May we now have the passing of the peace?" the minister asked. "Everybody rise. Embrace your brothers and sisters. Shake hands. Say good morning."

All around Jackson, people rose. Because Mrs. Simpson had been mentioned in the sermon, people made a special point of greeting Jackson. People he hadn't seen for years embraced him. Even ancient Mrs. Roberts who'd sicced the law on him in the sixth grade when he'd stolen her watermelons. And Mrs. Howard, the schoolteacher, who'd seen him streak naked through the town square on a dare from Logan.

And the more greetings Jackson received, the more his chest constricted. Maybe it was the peaceful atmosphere of the church itself. Or maybe it was just that Ellen was softening his heart, slowly but surely turning him into a more sensitive man. But a heartfelt longing to change his ways stole over him. And he decided he would never gamble again.

"Oh, Mrs. Simpson..." El was the last to give him a hug. "Isn't this wonderful?"

"It is," Jackson whispered back. He really meant it. And for the first time, he had real hope that things might come out right in the end.

6

"MRS. SIMPSON?"

Balancing an apple pie in one hand, Ellen knocked harder on the Simpsons' door. As it swung inward, she stuck her head through the crack. "Yoo-hoo. Is anybody here?"

She frowned. Only minutes ago, she'd dropped Mrs. Simpson off in the Land Rover. Remembering she'd meant to give the housekeeper the pie after church, Ellen had then rushed home, grabbed the pie, run down the hill and hopped the fence. But it seemed that Mrs. Simpson was already gone.

Cocking her head, listening for any sounds, Ellen felt a sudden sense of bone-deep unease. Something seemed out of whack. There was no vehicle parked down here, which was not surprising if Mrs. Simpson and Wyatt were out. But now that she thought about it, she realized she'd never seen any cars parked outside the Simpsons' home. How did Mrs. Simpson get to her other housekeeping jobs? And how did Wyatt get to work at Jackson West's ranch?

And would the Simpsons leave their door open? Well, maybe. Country people sometimes did; Ellen had found her own cabin unlocked—and only marginally vandalized. Still, she was used to New York and L.A. where open doors could mean a reign of terror. Venturing a step inside, she raised her voice. "Hello? Mrs. Simpson?"

Her pulse sped up. What if something had...
happened? She quietly set the pie on a living-room table, then peeked cautiously into the two bedrooms and
bath.

"She's fine," Ellen murmured, sagging in relief
against the door to Mrs. Simpson's bedroom. "She
must have just left."

Her position in the bedroom doorway gave her a
good view of the whole cabin. *In all its glory,* Ellen
thought with irony and a sudden twinge of bitterness.
It pained her that people as deserving as her friends
shouldn't have a more comfortable home. This place
reminded her of the apartment she'd once shared with
her father. The living room, while clean, was sparse
and shabby. The couch was worn, the floor uneven and
the TV was rigged with a makeshift antenna fashioned
from a coat hanger.

Suddenly a genuine smile curled Ellen's lips. Funny,
but the housekeeper who kept other people's houses so
neat and tidy wasn't so circumspect in her own most
private quarters. The navy suit she'd worn to church
was flung casually across the bed, and two wigs were
tossed on the dresser. The ironing board was up.

Well, now that she'd ascertained that Mrs. Simpson
wasn't home, she should go. And yet Ellen couldn't
help but stand there for a moment, feeling content to
be in the house of people who'd come to mean so much
to her. Her smile deepening, she wondered if she could
coerce Mrs. Simpson into dating minister Martin.

"You're such an inspiration," the widowed minister
had said at the church door, wringing Mrs. Simpson's
hand. "Maybe we could break bread together some
night?"

Ellen chuckled softly. *Break bread.* He'd really said
that. It had to be the most religious way that Ellen had

ever heard of asking a woman for a dinner date. She just hoped he didn't give up. When Mrs. Simpson declined, he'd said, "But please, I'm so impressed by the change in you."

"Oh, I'm changed, all right," Mrs. Simpson had snapped.

Not that she didn't have every right to be prickly around men, after her husband's suicide. But Ellen wished Jean would let herself begin to love again, as Ellen was doing herself. There were never lights on in the Simpson living room at night, though. Not even the glow of the TV. The Simpsons kept to themselves, as quietly as church mice.

Wyatt.

Ellen swallowed hard. His room looked almost unlived in. Staring at the neatly made bed, thoughts of the sexy cowboy lying in it came to her unbidden. More than once now, when he'd kissed her, she'd felt the full strength of his need. And remembering how his hard, insistent, aroused body pressed against hers, it was easy enough to imagine him in this bed—strong, virile and naked, ready to take her.

Pushing away the thoughts, Ellen's eyes strayed over his memorabilia, most of which was from high school. She guessed he'd been a good kid, active before his father died. There were trophies for wrestling, pennants for football games. A sadness stole over her when she thought of how the young man must have suffered when his father died so tragically—the way she'd suffered as her father drank himself to death. This room looked as if time had stopped for Wyatt, when his father died.

Poor guy. Words didn't come easily to him—unless he was flirting or talking about ranching. Well, the world of emotions was murky. Ellen would give him that. She hardly blamed a man for preferring the concrete realm where his dusty boot heels stayed firmly planted on mother earth.

He was passionate, though. His kisses proved it. So did the powerful urgency in his body when he held her. The thought of him—so tightly coiled and ready to spring—suddenly made her shudder. Should she ask him again to make love to her? "Why doesn't he try?"

The sudden ringing of a phone startled her. Glancing around, she thought it was the Simpsons', then she realized it was her portable. She drew it from her shoulder bag. "Hello?"

"Are you ready to talk?"

It was Abel again. "I need a few more days."

"Baby, you're costing time and money. We've got to start taking bookings, filling the calendar. And I'm about finished with the new stuff, which means I need your sorry butt in rehearsal."

Staring around Wyatt's room, Ellen felt something twist inside her. How could she tell Abel she didn't want to leave here? That all she wanted was to know the sexy cowboy next door—completely. The way a woman knew a man. "What about what *I* want, Abel?"

"I don't care what you want."

They both knew it wasn't true. "Please. I know this sounds corny, but I'm really…at a crossroads in my life."

"Crossroads?" Abel choked on the word. "I knew I never should have brought the band to the West Coast. Before we came to L.A., you didn't have this annoying need to find yourself. Your life had no crossroads. Baby, in New York, your life was a straight freeway. It was like I-5. Or U.S. Route One."

Yeah, and way back in Oklahoma, her life had been a maze strewn with grenades. But here in Montana, everything was starting to come clear. She felt grounded. Real. Wyatt was making her heart soar, yet bringing her down to earth. She finally sighed. "Well, Abel, now my life has crossroads."

He groaned. "Then step on the gas and get through the intersection a little faster, would you?"

"Sorry."

"What? Do you intend to stay stalled there forever?"

"Oh," she managed lightly, "you know me. I don't do things very gracefully, which means at the crossroads of my own life, I'll probably just wreck."

There was another long pause. Then Abel said, "Purity?"

Her lips curled. It had been a while since anybody had called her that. "Hmm?"

"I have faith in you. You won't wreck, baby. But don't stay stalled. I really need that voice of yours. It's too good to waste."

"Thanks."

"Don't mention it. Ciao, baby."

Sighing, she realized she was actually starting to miss Abel. And she didn't feel angry. For years, she and Abel had called their convenient, kissing friendship a romance—but it never could have been enough. Now she was just glad Abel had found a woman. Wasn't that the real reason she had fled L.A? Abel's romance had made her crave a love of her own—and craving love always made her bolt.

For so long, she'd loved an alcoholic father, and a mother who was nothing more than a˙memory. Not once had her love been returned. Now, wanting to be loved hurt too much. And yet, she desperately wanted love.

Beside her, on a dresser, she noticed a photograph

of jersey-clad football players. Picking out her blond, blue-eyed Wyatt in the middle row, she decided he was sexier now. Scanning the names in small print, she frowned. They were out of order; it seemed as if Wyatt had been identified as Jackson West.

She suddenly chuckled. If the typesetter had switched Wyatt's and Jackson's names, that meant Jackson had been the team's water boy. He didn't look a thing like the honey-haired, blue-eyed Wyatt. He had black hair and eyes, the beginnings of a mustache and a full mouth stretched into a friendly, good-natured grin. She could hardly imagine that cute kid growing up and ripping her off on a real-estate deal.

But he had. He was also a slave driver. Which was why Wyatt always had to work. Ellen never even got to see both Mrs. Simpson and Wyatt together—in one place, at the same time.

"This settles it," she said.

It was high time she visited Jackson West's ranch.

Ellen left a quickly scribbled note next to the apple pie. At the door of the Simpsons' cabin, she paused, taking a final glance around. Once again, that bone-deep unease hit her. Maybe later she would berate herself for not noticing all the little things: that Wyatt's bed had a wool blanket—when Wyatt had told her he was allergic to wool. Or that Mrs. Simpson had gone out, leaving two wigs behind—when she'd told Ellen she only owned two wigs. Or that Wyatt had said he'd brought her the double feather mattress from home— when the beds here were twins. Maybe she'd recall the faint scent of tobacco in the air—when she knew neither Wyatt nor Mrs. Simpson smoked. Or that she'd never seen Wyatt and his mother together. Yes, maybe later Ellen would think that the devil was always to be found in the details.

But for now, Ellen merely felt a vague creepiness. And then, whirling around decisively, she headed for the Bar Triple Cross and Jackson West.

"HEARD YOU WERE LOOKING for me."

Ellen glanced down at her T-shirt and jeans just as her favorite cowboy breezed through the back door. He was wearing threadbare jeans, a faded blue work shirt with pearl snaps and he smelled like a man—all sweat, hard work and dust. As he neared her, he whipped off his hat and sent it sailing onto the kitchen counter. Running a hand through his wind-tossed, hay-colored hair, he sent her a grin, just a quick, dazzling flash of teeth in sun-dark skin.

Ellen blew out a sigh of relief. "I was afraid you might be mad because I went up to Jackson West's."

He headed right for her. "We'll get to that, but..."

Just as he came up behind her, Ellen turned from where she'd been fixing a salad. He settled his hands on either side of her, resting them on the counter, trapping her. "You *are* mad," she said.

"Like I said, we'll get to that."

"But?"

"But we need to say a proper hello first."

Without any more warning than that, his lips came down on hers. The sound from her throat was hard to define—not quite a moan or a gasp or a sigh. From deep in his chest came an answering call—a low throaty rumble that met her on a level that had nothing to do with words. As his greedy lips began a slow savage plundering that warmed her whole body, her lips parted wider, inviting him inside, urging him to explore. Smelling him so close made her nostrils flare, and her heart hammered as she drew in a deeper breath of his scent. When his tongue delved deeper, she felt so giddy, she had no choice but to cling to him.

Seemingly sensing her need, he brought his hands swiftly around her waist, then his fingers strummed down the ridges of her spine, until his palms were molding her backside and slipping into the pockets of her jeans. When he squeezed, cupping her behind, pulling her against him, fiery heat spiraled to her core. Was this it? Would Wyatt finally take their physical relationship further? Her palms dampened against his nape, then raked upward, tangling in his hair. Arching against him, Ellen silently begged him to deepen the kiss that was already threatening to devour her.

But he knew how to tease and toy. And just when she was starting to ache for more, he drew back a fraction. His husky drawl sounded by her ear. "Now, that's a proper hello, sugar."

He'd left her feeling so sinfully sexy that on a breathless sigh, she said, "I don't know how *proper* it was."

He smiled. "It was a hello anyway."

Her heart was still beating a fast tattoo, and her voice matched his for raspiness. "If that's the way you say 'hello,' I don't think I can handle a goodbye."

His lusty chuckle had more than a hint of the devil in it. "Believe me, I'm not going anywhere."

"Good."

"So you think you can handle me?"

"Hey, cowboy, I'm a city girl."

"That just means you're not used to the call of the wild."

He couldn't have been more right, but Ellen assured herself he had no way of knowing it. "Maybe not, but I've been called wild on occasion. So I don't think you're going to throw anything at me I can't catch."

He kissed her quickly—all lips and tongue, coming and going in a flash, leaving behind nothing but heat.

"Missed me," he said.

While awareness danced in her veins, coursing through her whole body, her eyes dared him. "Want to try for double or nothing?"

For a heartbeat, his eyes turned dark. "Sorry, sugar, but my gambling days are done."

When he smiled, relaxing against her, it was almost too much for her. His chest felt too heavy, his maleness was too unmistakable. Beneath his casual demeanor, she could tell he was tensed and ready to spring. Especially when his dreamy blue eyes drifted down, lingering on her breasts. Surely he wanted her. A man didn't look at a woman like this unless he was thinking about making love.

As if reading her mind, he grinned. "So, you *really* think you can handle me?"

Maybe. "Yeah."

He squinted. "Are you mad?"

A little. His kisses had left her feeling edgy. "No. Are you?"

"No."

"Good." Wanting to change the subject, she said, "After church, I did go up to the ranch, but I was looking for Jackson West, not you. I figured it was about time I gave the man a piece of my mind. Not that I found him."

His expression seemed leery, strangely unreadable, to Ellen. "While you were raising hell about what he charged you for your property," he said "I guess you intended to throw in a word or two about how he underpays his employees, namely me."

Ellen flushed guiltily. A tough cowboy like Wyatt wouldn't want a woman meddling in his business. Contritely settling her palms on his chest, she slid them upward, the worn denim of his shirt feeling as soft as silk beneath her fingers. "I shouldn't have gone. But…well, you *should* be paid more. You see, I was down at your place after church, trying to catch your mom, since I'd baked you both an apple pie. And I just thought—"

"You were down at *my* place?"

She could swear she saw real concern in his eyes. "I left you and your mother a note. Didn't you get it?"

"Uh…I haven't been down to the cabin yet."

His eyes searched hers. What did he expect to see? Defensiveness crept into her tone. "I didn't snoop through your drawers, if that's what you're thinking."

"I didn't say that, El."

"And I only went inside because your mom didn't answer the door. I'd dropped her off just a few minutes before. I didn't see a car, and I knew you were working, so… I don't know…" She shrugged. "It just seemed weird. I thought she might have fallen or something. Or that maybe somebody had broken into the house. Anyway, she was gone."

"Maybe Marjorie or Bernadette came for her," he suggested.

Ellen nodded. That's what she'd finally decided. She sent him a conciliatory smile. "Well, I was just about to make steaks. Let's call and see if your mom wants to come up for dinner."

Just as she started punching the number in on her portable phone, his hand closed over hers. He pressed the Off button. His voice was sexy, irresistible. "Let's eat alone."

Let's not eat at all. She blew out a shaky breath. Didn't he guess his kisses heightened all her senses? At least she suspected that was the case. Because his eyes simply couldn't be this deep a blue. And his scent couldn't be this pungent. Or his body so hard and hot beneath his clothes. No, if he'd guessed how he affected her, he'd be touching her, loving her. A man couldn't realize he'd engendered this kind of ache in a woman—and not act. She swallowed around the dryness of her throat. "I'll just cook for us."

He lifted a hand and stroked her cheek. "I'm not mad about you going to the ranch," he said with a sigh. "Hell, even if I was, El, I couldn't stay mad for long."

She raised her eyebrows. "No?"

He shook his head. "I think you've found my soft spot."

She smiled, feeling pleased. "You've got one?"

Raising his thumb and index finger, he held them apart, just a fraction. "Yeah, but it's only about this big."

Ellen laughed. Poking at his ribs, she said, "Is it here?" She pinched his belly. "Or here."

"You're asking for it."

She grinned innocently. "For what?"

"You know what." His wry twist of a smile took the warning from his words. "Careful, El—or you'll get kissed again."

"I'm scared."

"You should be."

A heartbeat passed. "What? Lose your nerve, cowboy?"

"Look out for the big bad wolf." His warm lips seared hers again, and his tongue followed in a slow, wet kiss that went way beyond hello. Ellen gave in to the heady sensations—to his heat, his strength, her fingers curling on his shirt, catching denim in fistfuls. This time she drew away. She did feel scared now. Oh, she wanted him. She'd never wanted anything more. But for years, she'd run from men, sex and love. And heaven only knew how many healthy emotions. She wasn't used to wanting so much, to needing…

He was gazing deep into her eyes. One of his hands was still nestled in her back pocket; the other pushed a platinum lock from her face. "You've got hair like silk," he murmured.

She couldn't breathe. If they started making love, should she tell him she'd never done so before? Or should she do what she always had—pretend she knew the ropes? *Try one more time. Tell him you really like him, that you want to make love.*

Her lips parted, her voice sounded hoarse. "I *am* sorry," she said instead. "About going to the ranch. And anyway, I didn't even see Jackson. He was out, mending fences. But I met his mother and we had coffee."

He was staring at her. "Uh…you met his *mother?*"

She smiled. "Wound up staying about two hours. I met most of his family, I think. All his brothers—Austin, W.D., and Gary, and a sister-in-law named Crystal. I know he has sisters, but they weren't around."

Surely it was her imagination, but she could swear she saw a hint of panic in his eyes. Probably due to the meddlesome way she'd insinuated herself into the house of his employer. "I'm sorry I went there," she apologized again.

He said, "Well, what did you think of Marilla West?"

Ellen grinned. "I *really* liked her." Marilla West was a honey-haired, blue-eyed spitfire, as economical and quick in her movements as any cowboy. She rose daily at 4:00 a.m. to start cooking. As near as Ellen could tell, the woman regularly fed her kids, their spouses and half the cowhands. As well, Marilla handled the account books for the ranch.

She doted on her oldest son, too. Even Ellen's heart had softened a little when Marilla told her about the death of her husband—and how Jackson, then only eighteen, had given up his dreams of playing college football and studying agriculture, to tend to the ranch and support the family.

Ellen squinted, suddenly realizing that Marilla's eyes were the same shade of blue as Mrs. Simpson's and Wyatt's. She guessed maybe that was because so many people in this part of the country were of Germanic descent. His gaze had become cautious and watchful. "Why are you looking at me like that?" she said.

"Like what?"

Like you're afraid of what I'll do next. "I don't know." She shrugged. "Anyway, Marilla told me about the big Halloween dance tomorrow night." She smiled up at him. "Do you want to go? Marilla said there's a rental place in Silver Spoon that should have some costumes left."

The pause was so long, her smile faltered.

"Everybody in town goes," she added.

He looked vaguely preoccupied—or worried. "Yeah."

Ellen sighed. She knew from her conversations with the women from church that Wyatt had never really socialized much. "I know you haven't kept in touch with a lot of people in town. But you need to get out and mingle. I'll turn you into anything you want to be. C'mon, no one will even know who you are. You'll be in a costume."

His voice was strangely unreadable. "Guess you've got a point there."

"So you'll be my date?"

He looked so serious, he could have been wielding a scalpel during brain surgery, rather than contemplating going to a party. "Okay, sugar. I'll go."

She grinned. "Good. Hungry yet?"

"Starving. I'll fire us up a couple of steaks."

But he didn't move, merely ran his hand underneath her hair again and then delivered another kiss, nuzzling apart her lips, so his tongue could flicker against hers with velvet warmth. Other kisses had shaken her. Or scared her. Or warmed her at her core. This one made her mind dreamy and her limbs languid—as if she were no longer made of flesh and bone.

"I gotta say," he murmured, leaning away, "you're one hot lady."

And he was one hot man. She swallowed hard, poking his chest. "I'd better finish the salad."

With a soft pat to her bottom that stole away her last remaining breath, he moved around her, then pulled the steaks from the fridge. For a moment, they worked in silence, preparing the meal. And she wondered why he seemed so reticent about deepening their relationship. It was time. Past time.

He suddenly chuckled. "The way you're tearing at that lettuce, sugar, I'll need to put my salad under a microscope to find it."

She blinked. "I was just thinking."

"About what?"

"You."

"What about me?"

About how much I want you. She just couldn't say it. Dammit, she'd asked him to take her to bed once and he hadn't. She couldn't ask again. A woman had her pride. *Any more pride and you'll still be a virgin past your childbearing years.*

"You're going to hold me in suspense?"

As she started chopping carrots, Ellen decided to take another tack. "I've had a lot of men look at me. You know, when I sing."

His voice was dry. "I'll bet."

She glanced up. If she didn't know better, she'd flatter herself that the look was downright proprietary. A rush of pleasure tingled through her. "Jealous?"

"Let's just say I'd like to find all those guys who were looking and rip their eyes out." He grinned. "And then I'd go for the throat."

"Now that's civil."

He looked at her intently. Beneath their dreamy surface, those baby blues held something sharp and as incisive as the knife she was holding. He shook his head. "No woman has ever called me civil, sugar."

She sent him a quick smile. "You're more of a gentleman than you want to admit." *And I'm beginning to wish you were less of one.*

"Just don't tell anyone."

"I won't."

He edged closer. When he reached into the salad bowl for a slice of green pepper, she playfully slapped his hand away. "Quit."

"Man can't live by bread alone." When his eyes drifted over her, she was positive the innuendo wasn't all her wishful thinking. But then, years of looking too closely, of trying to anticipate her father's mood swings, had left her often reading too much into situations.

"Now, what were you saying about those men who love to look at you?" he continued. "You know, all the ones I have to go kill."

She shrugged. "I'm...used to people looking at me. But when you look, I always feel it. It...goes more than skin-deep." No look had ever made her feel so self-conscious. His eyes made her remember her full breasts and hips. And how—deep down inside—she was still such a little girl. Waiting to be discovered by a man. By him.

"When I look, El—" his voice had turned husky again "—it *is* more than skin-deep."

The words made her tremble inside. Her throat felt tight, her mouth dry. "Then...why are you always such a gentleman?"

"I'm beginning to wonder that myself."

Her breath catching, she looked at him for a long moment. She believed in him, she thought. She trusted him. He really wasn't like so many of the men she'd known. He wasn't a liar and a cheat. She settled a hand on his forearm. "Tell me, for real. How do you feel about me?"

They were in the realm of emotions again. "I...like you." His eyes cast around, as if he knew that wasn't enough. "I *really* like you."

She nodded, waiting.

"Aw, El," he added, "every time I look at you, I swear my stomach turns turtle."

It wasn't quite what she'd expected. On occasion, the man's country diction made her think she needed a good translator. "Uh...turn turtle? Is that good or bad?"

After a stunned moment, he chuckled. "Turn turtle," he said, "means my stomach's doing flip-flops. And I can't say if it's good or bad. All I know, sugar, is that it's making me feel crazy." He shot her a sexy, lopsided smile. "You know, like I've got bees in my bonnet."

Ellen's cheeks warmed. "Oh—" she sighed "—you don't even wear a bonnet."

"You'd be surprised."

His cryptic tone gave her pause, but she ignored it. With a soft chuckle, she said, "You definitely put bees in my bonnet, too."

As soon as the words were out, came a sudden, unbidden thought. *Just watch out, Ellen. Because bees always sting.*

7

JACKSON'S HEART was in his boots. And El was burrowed against his chest, snug as a bug in a rug. Digging
in his heels, he pushed them off in the porch swing;
even as his arm tightened around her shoulders, he was
damning fate for bringing them together, then damning
himself for being such a simple cowboy that he
couldn't resist her.

Could any man? Tonight, El had lit those countless
romantic candles on the upturned orange crate again,
and she'd brought out a portable radio and tuned it to
the soft country oldies she knew he liked. As his toe
tapped to Hank Williams's "They'll Never Take Her
Love From Me," Jackson decided maybe the worst
thing was that El didn't know how deeply she was
affecting him.

But he couldn't take his eyes off her. Not off her
face, which was the face of an angel. Not off the lush
pale mounds of her breasts that he had seen, rosy from
hot bathwater and covered with wet, scented bubbles
that caught the morning light. Nor could he ignore her
legs that were encased in tight black leggings right
now, but that he longed to see bare and parting for him.
And her wide brown eyes... The emotions in them
were like her personality, by turns innocent and then
knowing, vulnerable and then provocative. With only
a glance, she could put Jackson at the center of the

universe, making him feel as manly as a bull set loose in a cow pasture.

Jackson sighed in frustration. Hell, at this point, he had more thoughts on El Smith than Eli Whitney had ever had on the cotton gin. And a woman who was as worldly-wise as she was purported to be would have guessed it by now. No man looked at a woman the way Jackson looked at her, unless he had serious intentions. And no man kissed a woman so hard and deep, or with such regularity, unless he wanted her, body and soul.

If only he had played it straight. When she'd arrived in town, he should have knocked on her door, introduced himself as Jackson West and simply asked for her autograph, for the little girl in the hospital. *Yeah, and you wouldn't have gotten within a mile of here.*

Jackson was sure a lot closer than a mile now. And because he was accustomed to simply claiming what he most wanted and needed from a woman, his life was a living hell, his own damnable lies holding him back from Ellen. He really couldn't believe she still thought he was Wyatt Simpson.

She wiggled in his arms, tugging down the pearl-snapped denim shirt she wore that was identical to his, that had bunched beneath her heavy sweater. "Isn't it nice out here, Wyatt?"

He wished she wasn't still calling him that. His voice was low, almost a whisper. "Sure is, sugar." In spite of all his troubles, this was the kind of night he lived for—the autumn air cool and crisp, the sharp wind scented with pine and earth. A crescent moon, the same silver-white color as El's hair, hung in a sky of black liquid velvet that was scattered with a million brilliant stars. His voice deepened to a soft rumble. "Can't believe winter's right around the corner.... Thanksgiving and Christmas."

Settling her palm on his shirt, Ellen spread her fingers as far apart as they'd go, as if to see just how much of him she could touch at one time. She shrugged. "I don't care about holidays."

"You have to care about holidays."

She shrugged. "I don't have anywhere to go."

Jackson could have kicked himself. How could he have been so insensitive? Frowning, he tightened his arm around her back, his palm cupping her shoulder. "Where do you usually go?"

"I've got some girlfriends back East. I guess I could visit them. For the past couple of years, I've gone to Abel's parents' house in the Bronx, but now that he's engaged…"

Just thinking about El alone on a holiday made Jackson feel desperate to tell her about his family. She'd already met and liked his brothers, his mother and Crystal. And Darla would adore her. El would be welcome at the ranch anytime. Shoot, between all the nieces and nephews coming along these days, extra adult hands were always appreciated. It didn't hurt to have them on the annual trek up Miracle Mountain to cut a Christmas tree, either. Jackson suddenly smiled, thinking about all his family's good-natured bickering—how his sisters teased and his brothers roughhoused while his ma shooed everybody from the kitchen. Marilla wouldn't trust Santa Claus himself with her turkey.

"I'd love it if you could be with me for the holidays," Jackson wound up saying. El, with her mix of down-home good-heartedness and city-thick skin would fit in with the Wests as surely as boots fit into stirrups.

She smiled up at him. "For all the holidays?"

He smiled back. "Starting with Halloween."

"Hmm." The humming sound she made was as

warm as the cheek she pressed against him. "I wish...everything would stay just exactly like this."

He guessed she was worrying over the many things she'd left unresolved in L.A. "Me, too, sugar."

Some nights, Jackson even imagined himself, old and gray, and still sitting here, rocking with El on this very porch swing. Never before had he felt content to sit in near silence with a woman. Darned if he could figure it out, but these quiet nights had wound up making him and El closer than if he'd taken her on a hundred dinner dates. Gazing down, he noticed how the play of warm rose-amber candlelight made the platinum strands of her hair look like twined filaments of silver and gold. He didn't bother to hide the huskiness in his voice. "It's getting too cold for you to be out here. You ought to be careful of your voice."

She sounded almost drowsy, as if rocking in his arms was putting her to sleep. "You're keeping me warm."

"I want to keep you even warmer."

"Feel free."

"My pleasure."

Nestling farther into a corner of the swing, Jackson pressed a kiss to the top of her head. After a moment, she scooted up, and tucked her legs beneath her. Nuzzling a spot on his chest right over his heart, El started toying with his shirt, the way she always did, as if she spent half her time thinking about how to make him take it off.

"Should I run in and get a blanket?" she asked.

He shook his head. "Not unless you want."

"I want," she murmured. "But not a blanket."

The way her warm slender fingers were now slipping between his shirt snaps and teasing his chest hairs, made him feel downright warm. "You flirt," he accused gently. "Really, are you too cold, El?"

"If you'd hug me a little bit more, I'd be warmer."

He hugged her a little bit more.

Then she murmured, "So, what do you want to be?"

Your first lover, sugar. "Hmm?"

"For Halloween."

Halloween. A sudden attack of common sense had Jackson's lips parting, to back out of the date. It was risky and foolhardy—and it would only prolong his not telling her the truth. Which he had to do now. Pronto. But then, she wanted to go so badly. And she was right. Probably no one would recognize him.

"Hmm?" she prodded.

Jackson tilted his head as if considering, but really he was only looking at her. Her face was as bone white, smooth and dainty as the china cups he was getting so used to drinking from when he came around, dressed as Mrs. Simpson. And El used fine, expensive creams on her skin that made her hands and face silky soft. The parts of her that Jackson hadn't yet touched were probably as smooth as water.

"I don't know, El. What do you want to be?"

"If they have a costume, a fairy princess."

His smile faltered, and for the umpteenth time, he cursed the first day he'd put on Mrs. Simpson's orange-and-red flowered dress. He could still hear his sister Darla laughing, and he could hear her say, "Now, Jackson, we can't all be fairy princesses!"

He remembered the first time he'd seen El, too, pacing around the shack in her black lipstick, combat boots and sunglasses. She'd looked like a girl gangster on the run. Oh, she couldn't be unattractive in a thousand lifetimes, but Jackson knew she'd felt that way on occasion. Now she was all cuddly and made no effort to hide her natural sweetness. The more he'd gotten to know her, the more she'd made him change, deep inside. Had she changed, too? Is that why she wanted to be a fairy princess?

"I...want to wear a white dress. Something long, with a full skirt and a diamond tiara." She sent him a wry smile. "Okay, rhinestones."

He shook his head. "If anyone deserves real diamonds," he said solemnly, "it's you."

"Thanks."

"What did you wear last year?"

"Black face paint and a bodysuit with bones painted on it. I was a skeleton. The year before, I was a witch, with a pointy hat and a black leather miniskirt." She sent him a grin so wicked that his heart stuttered, and he was reminded that there was a whole other side to Ellen Smith. "I had thigh-high, spike-heel boots, too." She paused again, toying with his shirt snaps in a way that was starting to make him crazy. Then her voice caught. "But this year I want to be pretty, Wyatt."

Hearing the name Wyatt again brought Jackson back to reality—almost. But El felt so good, snuggled in his arms, that he quickly pushed the complications of their situation to the back of his mind. "You *are* pretty."

"Really?"

She knew she was. "Yeah."

Even though he was smiling, Jackson's throat felt tight. He knew she wanted to be pretty just for him. And she was going to wear white, like a virgin bride. He rubbed the sleeve of her sweater making it bunch beneath his hand, then made a show of smoothing it. "You'll look pretty as a picture."

When her hand dropped an inch, from his chest to his belly, he cast a quick glance down. Sucking in a breath, he decided she was getting awful close to his belt.

"So, what can I turn you into?" she asked.

Slowly but surely, she was turning him into a more sensitive man. "I'll be anything you want me to be."

"I like you just the way you are."

It was such a sweet flirtation. So innocent, it made him feel young again. "I guess you'll need a footman, sugar, to drive your coach."

She sent him a glance of reprimand. "I was thinking I might need a prince."

His heart hammered more than he wanted to admit. "A lying, cheating, scoundrel like me? I'm not fit to tie your shoes." That much was the truth.

She merely smiled. "Then it's a good thing glass slippers don't have laces."

"You really think you can turn an old frog like me into a prince, sugar?"

"Who knows? You'd have to quit leaping away."

Glancing down, he realized her hand had dropped to his belt buckle. Mesmerized, he watched a long slender index finger lightly, carefully trace the silver square, then the thick brown leather of his belt. About the tenth time she retraced that path, he felt hypnotized. And on fire. Even worse, El didn't seem to know how close she was to getting burned—and in more ways than one. But Jackson couldn't quite bring himself to rest his hand over hers and still her movements.

"I really need a prince," she murmured.

The words came like a natural reflex. "Then I'm your man."

His eyes sought hers in the candlelight. When her soft, vulnerable brown eyes meshed with his, her hand simply dropped again, gliding below his belt. Before he could stop her, he felt the heat of her fingers through his threadbare jeans as they curled boldly around the best and worst of him. With a silent oath and not-so-silent groan, he quickly slid his hand over the top of hers. Because he'd never felt so torn—wanting to make her stop that torturous pressure, yet wanting to teach her how he most liked to be touched—he kept holding her hand right where it was.

"I just wanted to…"

He knew exactly what she wanted to do. His mouth was as dry as sawdust. "C'mon, El—"

"Please."

The word he could have handled. But he couldn't take the raw need in her voice. Reflexively his hand squeezed, urging her fingers to close tightly around him, to really feel him. And then he swiftly turned, shifting his weight, nearly lifting her as he pulled her on top of him, so her arms sprawled on his chest and her legs straddled his thighs. Hungrily his hands raked up through her hair and, as the strands spilled through his fingers, he brought her lips crushing down on his. Drinking her in, using an unapologetic thrust of his tongue to boldly part her lips, he kissed her in a way he hoped would tell her all the things he couldn't say.

He knew he had defenses against a woman's body—even hers. That he wouldn't lose control immediately—even though the torturously warm spear of her untutored tongue was exploring him thoroughly now, even though his nostrils flared as her arousing natural musk edged from beneath the more delicate scent of her lotions and knifed into his lungs. Even when she fluttered wet kisses on his neck, he could handle her. He could enjoy the enthusiastic way her curious hand sneaked beneath his shirt snaps and teased thatches of chest hair. Not to mention how her pelvic bone crushed his groin, leaving him harder than he'd ever been.

But the emotions—Jackson wasn't sure he could handle those at all. El was making him as helpless as a baby. Every night now, he lay awake, imagining a life with her—babies and holidays and getting old. And then dawn would come, making him conscious of his empty bed. He wanted to see El beside him—to share a pillow, to tuck the covers around her bare shoulders.

Kissing her now, Jackson's tongue slowly, expertly, flickered inside her mouth—as if he was accustomed to these feelings of warring guilt and desire that were tearing him apart. As if his heart wasn't aching from wanting to love her, aching for things that hadn't even happened yet—and maybe never would.

Leaning back, he gazed into her eyes. And then, for the briefest instant, he did lose control. Before he even knew what he was doing, Jackson simply lifted her shirttail and pulled. Her sharp intake of breath made his pulse pound as the snaps popped open, sounding like a string of caps.

Her bra was black and lacy; pale mounds spilled from the cups and her skin peeked through in pretty patterns. Swallowing hard, Jackson didn't know whether to press a hand to her heart or his. "Oh, El," he whispered simply.

"Here," she whispered back, unhooking the front catch with trembling fingers, exposing her breasts to the cool night air.

"Oh, sugar…" Jackson wasn't sure, but he thought he heard his own voice tremble. "You're so beautiful." Full and ripe, she stole away his last remaining breath. And then he was completely gone. His hands were cupping her, exploring, gliding over, around and under the mounds. His mouth followed—slowly stroking the tips until they hardened against his tongue. Until her sharp cry of need brought him back to reality. He realized how close he'd come to losing the control he'd fought to maintain every moment around her. He was hard and aching now. Hurting with want. The breath that finally tore from him had a ragged edge.

Carefully he smoothed the cups of her bra over her breasts again and pulled together her shirttails. He was so gentle, he could have been touching glass, not denim. What the hell was he doing? El was a virgin. She deserved so much better than this.

She was still nestled between his legs, her hips tilted into him. Her mouth was slick and wet, swollen from kisses, her eyes glazed and warm. "Is it because I might leave?" she asked shakily.

What was she talking about? Jackson's heart was pounding so hard, he could barely concentrate. "Hmm?"

"The reason you don't want to sleep with me."

He could never let her think that. "Oh, I want to sleep with you."

"But you think because I have a career and travel..."

Maybe that was a part of what he felt. He knew country life could never be enough for her. Pushing back a lock of her hair, Jackson found his voice. "Well...there aren't many ads for heavy metal singers in the Silver Spoon free paper," he said gently. "There really isn't a lot for you here, El."

"You're here," she whispered back.

Those words, so softly spoken, moved him more than the physical crush of her body ever could. He was powerless to deny her anything that she wanted from him. Right now. Tonight. "Yeah," he whispered back, just as his strong arms closed tightly around her, pulling her possessively to his warmth. "I am here, El. Right here."

And now he would be her prince.

Jackson rose. And as he pinched out the candles, one by one, the porch got darker and the night grew still. He could swear the air felt denser, heavier with the importance of what he was about to take from her. And what he was about to give. He felt edgy, as if tonight was his first time, too. "If we don't put these out," he murmured, as if talking could settle his nerves, "we'll probably burn down the house, El."

"Maybe we're about to burn it down, anyway, huh?"

"We definitely generate enough heat between us, sugar."

Right now, he could feel the fire in her gaze. He guessed she wasn't going to tell him she'd never been with a man. It touched him that she was afraid to, that she'd rather let him think she was experienced and risk him being too rough, than risk him changing his mind.

But he was damn glad he knew. Sure, he had an unfair advantage—she'd told him things she'd only tell another woman. But for once, Jackson could use that for a good cause, to become her fantasy, her dream. When only the moonlight was left, Jackson switched off the radio. Everything was silent, save for the rustling of leaves and grasses and the creak of the rickety porch as he approached her. She gazed up sweetly at him from the swing. Towering above her, he felt strong, as tall and rugged as the ancient pines all around them in the mountains. Leaning down, he simply lifted her into his arms and cradled her against his chest.

"So romantic," she whispered, her breath warm against the neck her arms had so willingly circled.

Carrying her, Jackson toed open the door to the cabin, then kicked it shut behind them and headed straight for the bedroom. A shaft of moonlight fell through a crack in the curtains and onto the white comforter covering the old bed. As he laid her gently down and she sank into the feather mattress, the moon touched her hair. "You look like an angel on a cloud," he whispered huskily.

She blew out a shaky sigh. Then she sat up slowly, reached into a beside drawer and nervously handed him a box of condoms. He couldn't help but smile. It was a box of a hundred that she'd probably bought down at Bernadette's. "One will do," he murmured. *For now.*

Not that the comment relaxed her. A hitch of sound came from her throat, a nervous laugh that made him want to offer her a thousand reassurances. Instead, he concentrated on shrugging out of his jacket and removing the outer cellophane from the box. Then he set it aside and glanced up again.

His breath caught, lodging in his throat while his pulse thudded. El had gone ahead and removed her shoes, socks, sweater, shirt and bra. Taking one mindless step toward the bed, Jackson simply stopped again and stared, his heart swelling. She'd folded her clothes so neatly on the bed, as if not realizing that Jackson was about to muss those covers—and with her help.

His gaze roved over her breasts, the skin so pale in the dark, and then he took in how she was now sitting right on the edge of the mattress, with her hands anxiously clasped in her lap and her eyes as wide as saucers. Only her feet gave away that she was scared. Her toes—the nails of which he'd painted a soft pink just days before—curled silently, digging into the cold wood floor.

"Is there something you'd like me to do?" she whispered.

Lordy, her voice was tinged with fear, but what she offered was so sweet. Jackson didn't know if it was the question or the tone—but one or the other brought him to his knees. Literally.

He kneeled right in front of her and cupped her face, his thumbs tenderly stroking her cheeks. "I'll do everything," he assured her. All she'd have to do was lie back and learn how to enjoy the undivided attentions of a good man. "Don't be nervous. It's the first—"

Jackson drew in a sharp breath and continued. "Our first time together."

She nodded, but her eyes, although glazed with arousal, looked worried. Because she looked more like she was going to her death than to oblivion, which was where he was going to take her, it was all he could do to gather her into his arms. He delivered the kind of gentle loving kiss a prince gave his sleeping beauty. Or a husband gave a wife on a wedding night. As he deepened it, preparing her to enter the age-old dance of love, he eased away her jeans, then black silk panties that seriously threatened his control. Urging her back down on the mattress, he gazed into her eyes. His voice was low, raspy. "You've got to trust me, El."

Her voice was a mere croak. "I trust you."

But she didn't—not yet. So his tongue began another lazy trail around her breasts. His callused fingers stroked the hard peaking tips, letting her get used to the intimate caress, then to his tenderest suckling. Suddenly she cried out as the drizzle of his tongue moved slowly downward. By the time he was kissing her belly, his own shirt and jacket were off, his jeans unzipped. But he wasn't about to undress until he was good and sure that this first time would be everything El needed.

Sensing where his mouth was headed, she suddenly wrenched beneath him. "El," he protested silkily as he trailed kisses of fire on her belly, "I want to kiss you here…here…" His mouth inched down, his voice dropped huskily. "And here."

Her voice was wild. "No… I want…I want…"

She didn't know how to lie back and just accept the pleasure. He could barely find his voice. "Please," he finally ground out, "just hold on to me."

Her trembling, uncertain fingers obediently twined in his hair. She gasped—more in panic than arousal, he thought—as his hands slid beneath her hips. Swiftly, before she could protest, he lifted her to his lips like a full cup he was afraid might spill. And then his mouth settled over the sweetest thing he'd ever tasted. He was no good when it came to words about love. But this he did know. He had a gift for loving with his body, and passion that found no expression in words was expressed through his hands and lips and tongue.

And she did surrender.

As the long slow strokes of his tongue began to teach their unspeakable lessons, her hands that had clutched his hair began to smooth the strands. Her wrenching hips began to arch. Her nervous laugh became a moan so deep that it thrummed through him, shuddering as her flesh did in his palms. He loved her until her scent and taste drove him wild—until her warm skin dampened and until her heels dug into the mattress with a climax that brought her right into his arms. He hugged her tight, with all his strength, while soft whimpers fell on his ears, softer and sweeter than any music he'd ever heard.

In giving, Jackson had gotten more than he'd given. And it was too much for him. With her, he'd just found heat and joy he hadn't known was possible. And suddenly he realized what he most wanted—to make her love him so much that she would forgive him all his faults, and all his lies. He shucked off his pants. With the last remaining ounce of his control, he laid her back once more, found a condom and readied himself.

This time, her thighs parted like a soft sigh. He slid between them, his finger stroking her cleft just once. When he felt her honeyed response, a low moan rumbled deep in his chest. Wanting only to give her more pleasure, but knowing he could hurt her, he stopped, poised and ready to enter her. His little girl, he thought illogically. His woman.

She *was* his. With this act he'd claim her. And now he felt scared. "Look at me, El."

Her eyes were wide in the darkness. A sliver of moonlight from the window touched her face.

This just won't be right, he thought, *if I don't say the words.* "I love you."

She didn't say anything. But her eyes welled with tears. They didn't fall, just shone in her eyes, making the brown irises look as rich and deep as velvet in the moonlight. Suddenly Jackson's own eyes stung. He tried to tell himself it was just sweat. But he knew his heart was breaking for the little girl she once was. The woman she was now. And for the lover she was about to become.

In the next few minutes, Jackson discovered a restraint he didn't know he had left. Easing slowly inside the tight slick sheath of her, he took his time, helping her get used to the feel of a man. And not just any man—him.

And then suddenly it happened. Like magic. It was like all the most incredible things Jackson had ever known rolled into one: baby calves being born on crisp winter mornings, the last flickers of sunsets in the wide Western sky, and the snowcapped Montana mountains silhouetted by a silver moon.

Ellen's face, when she discovered the pleasure of it, was all those incredible things and more. Her legs loosened, like a ribbon from a gift, then wrapped around his back as naturally as breathing. And then, all at once, she was giving as good as she got. She was riding with Jackson toward the brink, driving so hard into the velvet dark that he could almost hear the thunder of hooves.

Their joining was deep and complete. When she came again, it was with a woman's body—damp and hot from the ride, pungent with erotic scents; she was clinging to him with all her heart.

Only then did Jackson give in to the darkness. He slipped over the edge soundlessly, with quiet stoicism—like the cowboy he was. But still waters ran deep. And as his mind went black, his last thought was that after all these years of wanting, he'd really fallen in love. Ellen was the right woman.

After this he'd never take another.

THROUGH THE WINDOW, the moist, dew-filled air was still more gray than rose, though birds were starting to sing.

Ellen wanted to sing.

After all, there was a naked man in her bed—finally. Reverently she tucked the covers around him and smiled. It was funny how a few hours could change your entire life. She felt so…normal. At peace. So completely healed. Suddenly changing her mind, she mussed the covers again, snuggling beneath them, smelling him, rubbing her cheek against his chest, letting the golden chest hairs tease her skin. She wondered if she should wake him. After all, he'd have to get out of here before his mother arrived.…

She suddenly realized he was already awake—and that she was being watched by lazy blue eyes. Hot warmth made her cheeks tingle. In the light of day, she wasn't quite sure what to say. "You know, I'd never…done it before," she whispered.

He merely sent her a lazy smile and trailed a finger down her cheek. "No kidding."

Her smile took the sting from her accusation. "You guessed."

He didn't answer, only drew her closer and kissed her. Sighing against his mouth, she let her palm slide effortlessly down his side. Last night she'd expected the physical release. But the emotions surprised her. Sure, she'd wanted to run. But all night long, this man had held her fast. And this morning, she loved him for that patience. For his silences. And because he was a straightforward cowboy who couldn't fake his emotions.

Not that she believed he loved her in a permanent way. But it had meant so much when he'd said the words. It had been so many years since she'd heard them. Ellen only vaguely remembered her mother saying, "I love you," before she'd died, and Ellen's father never had.

I love you.

She could still hear those wonderful words, spoken in a soft soul-warming drawl. Hearing them last night had meant the world to her. So had the way he'd kept reaching for her. Guiding her, he'd urged her to explore her womanly power over him. He'd loved her so many ways. All night long. And even now he was ready for her. Reaching beside the bed, he found a condom. Facing him, gazing into his eyes, she let him slip inside her like a dream that would never end.

"Good morning, sugar," he drawled throatily.

"Morning, yourself," she whispered back.

And then his searing lips closed over hers once more. With a shuddering sigh, Ellen let her eyes flutter shut, surrendering completely. She could barely believe she'd found him, this cowboy who'd made a woman of her. As heat suffused her limbs, her arms circled his neck—the proof that it was true. He was here. He was hers.

And his name was Wyatt Simpson.

8

WYATT—THE REAL WYATT—glanced around the conversational groupings of sofas in the lobby of Silver Spoon Memorial's rehabilitation wing, as if he still couldn't believe his ears and was searching for a witness to corroborate Jackson's story. "Are you crazy, Jackson?" he finally burst out. "What do you mean my mother and I have become an inspiration to the whole community?"

The younger man's bright dark eyes were no longer bloodshot, his black hair had been restored to a glossy sheen, and his mustache was freshly trimmed. His starched white, button-down shirt was tucked neatly into clean blue jeans, and his boots gleamed from recent polish. These days, Wyatt Simpson was looking a whole lot better than Jackson West felt. "You heard me."

"But, Jackson—" Wyatt gripped the edges of the lobby couch, as if to brace himself "—the simple truth is that hard drinking runs in my family. My mother drank—and my dad, too! There wasn't any star-crossed love triangle or tragic suicide, the way everybody in town says. My dad died in his sleep. He never even owned a gun. Because I was eighteen when he died, mom said I was old enough to be on my own. Then she simply left town, without even packing her bags. But she ain't dead. At least not as far as I know."

"Not dead?" Jackson echoed.

Wyatt glared at him. "No!"

"I mean, I'm glad to hear it," said Jackson. And he was. He just hoped Mrs. Simpson didn't come back to town anytime soon. "Do you know where she's living?"

"No, I do not! And what do you mean, you've been dressing up in the dresses my mother left behind when she moved?" Suddenly Wyatt's jaw went slack and he merely stared, shaking his head in horror as if he'd never seen Jackson before. "And you think *I've* got problems? *You* threw *me* into the rehab section of a psychiatric ward? Phew! If this isn't the pot calling the kettle black. Jackson, you've obviously got more than one screw loose. I'd better call a nurse for you—"

"Please, Wyatt. Just calm down."

Instead, Wyatt shot off the couch like a rocket from a cannon and started pacing. "Don't you dare tell me to calm down! You've got some nerve. You absolutely cannot go around town—the same town where we were born and raised and where everybody knows us—wearing my mother's old dresses!"

"I know that!" Jackson exploded. "That's why I came here, to ask for your help. Look, it was just a bar bet...a joke that went too far."

Wyatt plopped down again on the couch opposite Jackson. Leaning forward, he knitted his black eyebrows together and stared at Jackson, hard. "A joke? You *really* think this is funny?"

"No, I—"

"Well, it's not funny, so I suggest you lie back on that couch where you're sitting, Jackson. Yes, you'd better relax, shut your eyes and get comfortable. Because what you obviously need is a good therapy session."

"At this point, I'm half inclined to agree with you, but—"

"Don't you even *talk* to me!" Wyatt exploded again, suddenly wagging his finger in Jackson's face. "Just let me get this straight. Because of a bar bet you made with Logan Hatcher, you've really been dating Ellen Smith? Purity? The lead singer for the Trash Cans?"

Jackson couldn't help but feel pride at El's success. And relief, since Wyatt was finally calming down enough to let him respond. "You've heard of them?"

"Everybody's heard of the Trash Cans!" Wyatt exclaimed, sounding mad all over again. "And don't you dare try to sidetrack me."

Suddenly feeling worn-out, Jackson lifted his tan Stetson by the brim, swept it off, then ran a hand distractedly through his hair. He set the hat beside him on the couch. "Look, I came because I need a favor."

"Oh, no. If you think you're going to involve me in this—" Wyatt swiftly reached into his shirt pocket and whipped out a small black nurse call device and began frantically pressing the button. "Nurse!"

Jackson gasped. "What do you think you're doing?"

Wyatt sent him a long level look. "Given everything you just told me, I think I must be sick again. I must be having a relapse. Please, Jackson," he said, "tell me I'm having delirium tremens."

"I wish you were," Jackson said grimly. "But unfortunately, everything I've told you is the truth."

Giving up, Wyatt sighed and waved away the nurse who was fast approaching. "You just wait till your sister Darla hears about this wild stunt you've pulled."

"Darla knows."

"Darla? *My* Darla?"

Jackson's eyes widened. "What do you mean? *Your* Darla?"

Wyatt crossed his arms, looking vaguely defensive. "Well, I didn't have any family to come for the family group therapy sessions, so the counselor said I could ask a friend to sit in. And since Darla knew I was here, and was nice enough to visit me regularly, I asked her...." Wyatt suddenly smiled. "When I get out, Darla says we can start dating. Of course, it'll just be casual, maybe not even kissing—at least not during the first year of my sobriety."

Jackson could merely stare. *What have I done?* All his big-brother instincts were on red alert. Was his baby sister, Darla, really going to date Wyatt? Wyatt—who'd been laid up in bed for the past few years, drunker than a skunk? Even worse, from the dreamy quality in Wyatt's dark eyes, this was a serious romance. This boy was thinking marriage.

"I've had a crush on Darla since grade school," Wyatt said wistfully. "But I had low self-esteem, so I never could get up the nerve to ask her out. Darla and I talked about it with the therapy group."

Jackson sighed. He wanted to say, *No offense, Wyatt, but I was trying to get you sober—not wind up related to you.* But then, Jackson didn't want to jeopardize Wyatt's newfound self-esteem, so he kept his mouth shut.

Sensing hesitation, Wyatt stared at him stoically. "I'm changing my life now, Jackson. I'm going to make something of myself. Darla's safe with me. And tomorrow I'm getting out of here—"

"Which is exactly why I came," Jackson quickly interjected. "Now, tonight Ellen and I have a date for the Halloween dance..."

Wyatt moaned in protest. "You have to tell her the truth! Are you off your rocker?"

That Wyatt Simpson was fast becoming the sole voice of sanity in his life was something Jackson hardly wanted to contemplate. He grimaced. "Look, I'm going to tell her the truth, but—"

"When?"

Good question. "Soon. The thing is, she can't find out the *whole* truth. I sure don't want her to know I pretended to be your mother, wore dresses every day and took the housekeeping job."

Wyatt's voice was as dry as melba toast. "Well, I can't blame you there."

"Please," Jackson said. Wyatt had to help him. If he would, maybe El wouldn't be too mad. *El.* At just the thought of her, Jackson's heart fluttered. The woman had gotten him in touch with his sensitive side, all right. Nowadays, he couldn't have two consecutive thoughts without her appearing smack-dab in the middle of them. He'd never known what he was missing, or how much of his life it was possible to share with a woman. Before he'd met Ellen, he was like a house closed up for winter. He knew that now. His doors had been closed, his windows shut, his shades drawn. Then Ellen had come along and opened him up. Now, everything seemed to flow inside him—she went in and out of his soul freely, through all the open doors and windows, like a sweet breeze.

"What about Logan's land?"

Jackson blinked. "Hmm?"

"Did Logan give you the deed? I know you've been trying to get that property for years."

Jackson shot Wyatt a look of censure. "Forget about that deed. I'm just worried about Ellen."

Wyatt wolf whistled. "Let me get this straight. You care less about winning that bet with Logan and getting that land than about Ellen Smith?"

Jackson was in love with her, pure and simple. "Of course I do. Now, Wyatt, when you get out of here tomorrow, I want you to do me a huge favor. From now on, you've got to pretend your mother had to leave town, to take care of a sick sister in Denver—"

"My mother doesn't even have a sister."

Jackson groaned. "That's not the point."

Wyatt merely raised an eyebrow. "Okay. So, you want me to pretend my mother has been called away, to care for a sick relative?"

Jackson nodded. Now, Wyatt was catching on. At least this plan would give Jackson a fighting chance. "Tomorrow morning, I'll go to El's dressed up—"

Wyatt rolled his eyes in protest. "In one of my mother's dresses?"

Jackson ignored Wyatt, thinking out loud. "Yes. I'll explain that I have to go away because my sister's sick in Denver. And then later in the day, when you get your walking papers from here, you and I will visit El together. We'll introduce *you* as the real Wyatt Simpson—"

"Which I am," Wyatt reminded him flatly.

"Right." Jackson nodded. "And we'll explain that you were so embarrassed about your drinking problem that you didn't want anybody to know you were in the hospital. So, when your mother needed to get a handyman for Ellen, she couldn't say you were in the hospital. See?"

Wyatt looked appalled—as if he didn't see at all.

Jackson forced himself to continue. "Because you were unavailable, your mother asked me—Jackson West—to fix up El's house."

"Because I was really in the hospital?" Wyatt clarified.

"Uh-huh. And because Ellen was mad at me, because I, Jackson West, had sold her that lousy piece of property, I then introduced myself as you." Jackson squinted, thinking hard. "By introducing myself as you, you see, I made everybody happy—"

"How thoughtful of you, Jackson."

Jackson glared at Wyatt, then continued. "Since El thought I was you, nobody guessed you were in the hospital, which would have embarrassed you. I got to start making amends to Ellen, by rehabilitating her shack in my spare time. And, of course, Ellen got a habitable place to live." *And then we fell in love. And the rest is history.* Jackson sighed in sudden relief. He thought that sounded reasonable.

Wyatt didn't look convinced. "This is awfully complicated, Jackson."

"True," Jackson admitted. "But if you think it through slowly, it does make sense." In fact, it very neatly tied up all the loose ends.

"Wouldn't telling the truth be easier?"

"Of course."

"Then why go through all this rigmarole?"

"Because if I tell the truth, she'll never speak to me again."

"Good point," agreed Wyatt. After a long silence, he frowned. "I *am* grateful to you, Jackson. After Daddy died and my mom left, you know what I was like. Without you, I would have wound up on the streets. When nobody was there to help me, you kept a roof over my head and food in my belly. Then you threw me in here and helped me get sober, too. And I quit smoking. And I'm dating your sister.... Really, I guess I don't rightly know how to thank you—"

"Please don't say a word," Jackson said quickly. He didn't mind doing the occasional good deed, but it embarrassed him to talk about it. "I would appreciate it, though, if you could help me out of this jam."

"Honesty is a big part of my recovery program," Wyatt said, looking torn.

"I love her," Jackson said softly.

Wyatt nodded. "Well, I do owe you a lot—absolutely everything, in fact. I've got a whole new lease on living now. So, for you, Jackson, I figure I can tell one little white lie."

Jackson grabbed his hat and rose to go. "Thanks."

"And, Jackson?"

"Hmm?"

"Girls always went nuts for you, but I never saw you smitten before. From the look on your face, you've got it bad. So, for your sake, I sure hope this plan of yours works."

"Me, too, buddy," Jackson whispered. "Me, too."

"Care for more punch, sugar?"

Ellen shook her head, and glanced around the Miracle Mountain dance hall. The hall was dim, lit only by candles nestled down in pumpkin-shaped holders on the tables. Glow-in-the-dark skeletons and ghosts glowered from the walls, and black and orange streamers hung from the ceiling. It was getting late, the fast numbers were over, and now costumed couples swayed to slow country love songs. Gazing into his eyes, Ellen murmured, "No, I'm fine. Let's just dance again."

He leaned close, his breath teasing her neck, his soft drawl warming her blood. "Anything your heart desires."

"This time, can I lead?" she teased.

"Sure."

But on the dance floor, he took control, wrapping her tightly in his embrace, burying his face against the slender column of her throat, settling his palms on the small of her back. Wreathing her arms around his neck, Ellen sighed. Everything about him stirred her blood—the warm pressure of his thighs, the wedge of his foot between hers, the touch of his lips against her skin. "Wyatt," she suddenly whispered. "My Wyatt."

She felt beautiful tonight. For her fairy princess costume, she'd rented a bridal gown with a fitted lace bodice, long sleeves and full skirt. In a dime store, she'd found a crown-shaped rhinestone tiara. Because her favorite cowbay had insisted he wanted to be "tall, dark and handsome," she'd found a black wig to obscure his blond hair, which she'd tied back in a princely ponytail, and had added a black paste-on mustache and a mask that hid his eyes. Leggings, an aristocrat's jacket and a wide-brimmed hat with a white plume completed the costume. Strangely, he'd wound up looking like the water boy in the football picture in his room. If Ellen hadn't known who he really was, she'd never have recognized him tonight.

"At least we made it here," she murmured.

He chuckled huskily. "No thanks to you."

She laughed. This man was bringing out things in her that she'd never guessed she had. Tonight she'd played the good girl. The bad girl. And now she knew she wanted to be every kind of girl in the world for him. "You loved every minute that we were late."

"I sure did."

Tonight, when he'd come over to dress in the costume she'd rented for him, he'd caught her still in the tub. He'd wound up climbing right into the bubbles with her, naked except for his hat. She'd never imagined the kind of loving that had followed. Later, as she'd stood back to survey her dress, clad only in her garter belt, white stockings and high heels, he'd wrapped his arms around her again—and shown her what all those sexy clothes she'd been wearing for years were really made for. It was so wonderful that she wasn't even going to worry about the one condom that had broken.

Now Ellen grinned up at him. "Dressing up is fun," she teased, "but undressing sure is funner."

Throaty laughter rumbled in his chest. "I'm not much with words, sugar, but even I know *funner* ain't good English."

"It ain't, cowboy?"

"Nope." His teeth flashed white, as he grinned in the dark. "And I'm no cowboy. In this costume, I get to be a prince instead of the scoundrel I really am."

She smiled, thinking of how wicked he'd made her feel in the bubble bath tonight. "I like it when you're a scoundrel. And I like you dressed in anything. Though as little as possible is best."

"You sure learn quick," he murmured approvingly, dropping a string of warm, damp velvet kisses along her neck. "Speaking of costumes, have I told you yet you look beautiful in that dress?"

Ellen laughed softly. "At least a hundred times."

"And did I mention you smell so good I could eat you up?"

She nodded. "Hmm. Two hundred times. For the strong, silent type, you're becoming a real talker."

"Oh, sugar," he drawled, "you've loosened my tongue." Squinting at her, he looked perplexed. "Wait. Did I tell you that you look beautiful?"

She laughed. "Just a second ago."

"Good. And what about how you taste?"

His words heated her blood, warmed her cheeks. "What about it?"

"Well, if I happened to forget to mention that you taste better than candy," he whispered huskily, licking at the sweet confection of her skin, "then I want to say it a thousand times."

"If you say it a thousand times," she replied, her own voice a mere rasp, "it'll be too late when we get home to—"

His quick, lusty chuckle curled her toes. "Now *that* would be a shame."

With a shudder of anticipation, Ellen tightened her arms around him, shutting her eyes. As they turned in a slow circle on the dance floor, she reveled in the heat shimmering through her veins. For the whole next song, they were quiet. Everything seemed to disappear. There was only her and him—and the unstoppable sparks that flared between them.

"Hey there, Wyatt. Good to see you."

Ellen glanced up, but her date didn't bother to move his head from where it was burrowed against her neck, though he lifted a hand from the small of her back and waved. Ellen squinted through the darkness at the speaker who was tall and broad, and dressed as a hobo. The woman dancing with him wore a ghost costume.

"I'm Ellen," she said to the couple. "Ellen Smith."

Still dancing, the couple introduced themselves as Logan Hatcher and Judy Williamson. Over the music, Judy and Ellen chatted for a minute.

During a break in the conversation, Ellen lowered her voice. "You know, you could be more sociable," she whispered, not really caring that he wasn't.

"Why would I mingle—" he whispered back, a strange hint of gruffness in his voice "—when I want you all to myself?"

"Well," said Logan with a friendly chuckle, the next time he and Judy danced close, "you can bet my buddy Jackson West is madder than a hornet about you dating Wyatt here."

Ellen's eyes narrowed. "I don't even know Jackson West. Why would he have any feelings about me dating Wyatt?"

Logan laughed easily. "Oh, there's a piece of land up by you that Jackson's been trying to get for years. So, when you came into town, we struck up a bet that if he slept with you, I'd give him the deed to the property." Logan laughed again. "Of course, everybody knew he didn't have a chance."

Everybody? Ellen could merely stare. She felt herself being maneuvered away from Logan and Judy, but she pulled back. Peering over his shoulder, she said,

"Jackson West made a bet that he could *sleep* with me?"

Logan shot her a grin in the dark. "Yeah. And now that you and Wyatt are an item, he must be eating his heart out."

"Well, he did get the autograph and the corset for Dusty," said Judy, and filled Ellen in on the details before another couple danced between them.

"Did you hear that, Wyatt?" Ellen whispered.

"Yeah," came the soft murmur against her neck.

She suddenly frowned, trying unsuccessfully to lead them back toward Logan and Judy. If she didn't know better, she'd swear that her date was trying to dance to the other side of the room.

"Well, I don't remember signing any autographs," she whispered. Had Jackson West forged her name, passing his own signature off as hers? From what little she knew about him, Ellen wouldn't put it past him. Maybe he'd bought a corset, too, and then claimed it was hers. "Wait a minute. Wyatt," she said, "where did you put that bag of clothes you threw away?" Was it her imagination or did he stiffen against her?

He shrugged. "Uh, I just took it out...."

Forcibly Ellen took the lead and danced him back toward Logan and Judy. "Is Jackson here?" she demanded.

"Haven't seen him," said Logan. "And look, I didn't mean to ruffle your feathers. Believe me, it was all in the spirit of fun. The autograph was for a little girl named Sandra Sullivan who's in the hospital in Silver Spoon. She's only twelve and she's a big fan of yours."

"Jackson's not a bad guy," Judy quickly put in. "Just a little wild. You know, a little too macho for his own good. We shouldn't have told you."

"Sorry," Logan said again. "But look at the bright

side. Everybody's heard you're dating Wyatt, so Jackson's probably in hiding.''

''And I mean to force him out of the woodwork,'' Ellen fumed. ''Why does everybody keep protecting him? He's a rich rancher. Probably an abusive employer. And he plays dirty in the real-estate market.'' She suddenly stilled her steps, her voice rising. ''And now I find out that he made a bet about sleeping with me! How positively vile!''

''El?''

''*That's* it,'' she said flatly.

She didn't know which she felt more—furious or mortified. What was wrong with men? Did they really think these stunts they pulled were cute? Spinning on her heel, she darted straight for the door.

Just as they reached the exit, a bright white light flashed in her face. Rapidly blinking, Ellen made out a cameraman lingering in the shadows. He was probably from *Rolling Stone* or *Music Beat*. She'd thought all those people had left town, so maybe this guy was local. Whoever he was, the fact that she was still under scrutiny made her even angrier. Ignoring the man, she pushed through the door.

''El...'' She felt a warm hand on her back, steering her in the direction of a parked truck. ''Where are you going?''

''To find Jackson West.'' She didn't care if she was wearing a fairy princess costume; she was going to hunt him down.

''And do what?''

''Kill him.''

''HOLD YOUR HORSES, SUGAR.'' Jackson came to a standstill in Silver Spoon Memorial Hospital's crowded parking lot and tried to disengage Ellen, whose fairy princess costume was snagged on the side-view mirror of a Toyota. She was as riled up as a hellcat. Her teeth were clenched, chiseling her jaw into such a fiercely determined line that Jackson could swear he'd seen softer granite in a rock quarry.

She tried to move forward. "I don't know why you keep defending Jackson."

Sighing, Jackson freed the white gossamer fabric from the mirror, then shrugged out of his jacket and slipped it around El's shoulders. The gesture left him wearing a shirt that was far too ruffly for his taste. But he'd live. Hell, this was nothing compared to dressing as a woman. "Sugar," he finally said, "I'm not protecting Jackson. I just hate to see you make yourself crazy like this."

Ellen merely crossed her arms over her white gown. "Well, I'm sorry Jackson West ruined our evening, but I have every right to be mad."

Jackson couldn't agree more. "You do."

And then he sighed again. Because he'd feared someone at the dance would recognize his truck, he and El had had to walk a half mile to his parking spot. After that had come some fancy footwork. He'd stopped at Dusty's—fortunately everybody was at the Halloween dance—and Ellen had run inside to see if the moose above Dusty's bar was really wearing her corset, which it was. Then, getting pricklier by the minute, she'd made Jackson drive to the ranch. Parked in his own driveway, he'd watched her run inside to ascertain that Jackson wasn't there, which of course, he wasn't.

And now they were at the hospital, so Ellen could visit Sandra Sullivan and take a good look at the autograph. Each time he tried to dissuade her from going inside, Ellen simply glared at him so meanly that he could have been Jackson West. *Which I am,* Jackson thought with a sudden start. Lordy, shuffling all these identities was really getting to him. Staring at Silver Spoon Memorial, Jackson wondered if he shouldn't just check himself in.

"Wyatt, are you going inside with me or not? I need your support."

"Of course I'm going." He just hoped they didn't run into Wyatt—the real Wyatt. Or that Wyatt wasn't paged over the intercom.

Lifting her full white skirt off the pavement with one hand, Ellen grabbed his hand with the other. "Well, then, c'mon."

Twining his fingers with hers, Jackson let her lead him around the parked cars, wondering what had gone wrong. One minute they'd been dancing like the happily-ever-after prince and princess they were meant to be. And the next minute, his princess was dragging him off on a homicidal mission. Thank heaven by this time tomorrow, if his plan worked, this would all be over.

As he and Ellen charged through the electronic double doors of the hospital, people in white lab coats glanced up from their work and stared, making Jackson wish he were dressed in something other than a prince outfit.

Ellen stopped at the front reception desk. "I'm looking for a little girl named Sandra Sullivan."

The receptionist squinted at El. "Oh, heavens, it's Purity! Everybody's talking about you, saying you bought a cabin in Miracle Mountain. My son listens to your music—he's fourteen." The woman lowered her voice. "It's so nice of you to come visit little Sandra. She was thrilled by your autograph. I think everybody in the hospital's seen it."

For a minute, as Ellen put her anger on hold and played celebrity, Jackson felt a quick tug of unease. He realized if he and El stayed together, he'd always have to share her. For the first time, he wasn't ahead of the game in a relationship, or even on a level playing field. The best he could hope for was that Ellen would forgive him, and settle for a simple cowboy. In return, he'd do anything to help her career. Insofar as sharing her went, he'd manage somehow. He wanted everything with her—a lot of time and a family. But he'd probably settle for less, for whatever she was willing to give. The fact was humbling.

"Well, it's after visiting hours," the receptionist finally murmured, as Ellen signed an autograph for her son. "But Sandra will be so incredibly thrilled, so here's a couple of special, after-hours' passes."

"Guess that's my first taste of celebrity clout," Jackson murmured in the elevator, holding Ellen against him.

"Bother you?"

"Not in a way I can't handle."

"Good," she whispered. "Wyatt?"

Even as he lightly stroked her cheek, Jackson felt a sudden, unexpected rush of temper. Damn. He wanted to hear her speak his name—his real name—just once. "Hmm?"

"I'm sorry I'm taking this out on you."

His heart suddenly ached. If she knew the awful things he'd done—and if he had his way, she never would—then she'd have every right never to speak to him again. At the mere thought of losing her, Jackson pulled her closer. "You can take it out on me all you want." Lord knew, he deserved it.

Leaning back in his arms, Ellen gazed into his eyes for a long moment. When she stretched and kissed his cheek, the soft touch of her lips was the sweetest thing he'd ever felt. "I'm just glad I found you," she whispered.

The implication was that he was a better man than Jackson West. "Me, too, sugar."

"The whole idea of that bet just makes me sick."

Jackson couldn't believe he was in the horrible position of having to commiserate with her about what a bad guy and miserable cuss Jackson was. "It's awful," he forced himself to say. And it was. He just wished there was some way he could assure her he'd given up gambling for good.

Fortunately, before she could say more, the elevator doors swooshed open. They headed down the hallway of the pediatrics ward and within minutes had located Sandra's room, the door to which was decorated with pictures of pumpkins and ghosts.

At the sight of Sandra, the rest of Ellen's anger seemed to vanish, and Jackson actually grinned. Sandra was adorable, with two shiny chestnut braids hanging over the shoulders of her pink ruffly pajama top.

"I can't believe you came to see me," she gasped. "And you're dressed in costumes! Oh, I wish Mommy and Daddy were still here. They had to go to the motel, 'cause visiting hours are over. Oh, they're never going to believe this!"

"I was wondering how you've been," said Ellen.

Sandra grinned. "I'm not even sick anymore. After the car wreck, I was in ICU for a while, but now they're just keeping me here for physical rehab." She flung back the covers, proudly exposing a brace on her leg.

Before Ellen could respond, the little girl continued, her eyes shining with excitement. "I'm s'posed to be asleep, but I've been here for more than a month now, so I get to stay up late sometimes. In two more weeks, I should be as good as new. And then I get to go home."

Laughing, Ellen fussed around her. Jackson couldn't help but keep smiling. He guessed, like him, Ellen had a soft spot for kids. He listened as the two talked about music and Sandra's hospital stay. The only hint El hadn't come solely out of concern for Sandra's health was the careful way she scrutinized the autograph.

"Daddy and Mommy had it framed for me," Sandra explained, pointing above her bed. The signature Jackson had acquired from Ellen on his first visit to her cabin was matted and displayed in a small white frame decorated with pink hearts. Ellen seemed to recognize her own handwriting, but she seemed unable to recall when she'd signed the paper.

"Well, it's getting late," Ellen finally murmured when a nurse arrived, saying it was past bedtime. "What do you say—my friend and I will tuck you in. Okay?"

Sandra sighed sleepily, resting on her pillows as contentedly as if a lifetime dream had been fulfilled while El tucked the covers around her. Ellen murmured, "Ready for your lullaby?"

Sandra smiled. "You're the best."

Jackson's breath caught. He couldn't have agreed more. El was one hell of a woman. For someone who hadn't had much mothering, herself, she was incredibly maternal with this little girl. For the umpteenth time, Jackson hoped his own plans worked. They had to. He couldn't live without this woman. One last time, he'd put on an infernal dress. He'd end his career as Mrs. Simpson. Then, after he and Wyatt talked to her, he'd have to pull out his every last trick and charm El, so she'd forgive him the rest.

Sandra whispered, "No one'll ever believe a big star came to see me."

"Sure they will," Ellen whispered back. "After all, you're a star yourself."

Sandra giggled. "I am not a star."

"All little girls are stars," Ellen assured her.

The next thing Jackson knew, he was seated behind

Ellen on the bed. And soft and low, as if his life depended on it, he found himself whistling backup, as Ellen sang "Twinkle, Twinkle Little Star."

As her soft rich voice harmonized with his whistle, Jackson's eyes drifted over her gossamer white gown, the skirt of which was spread on the covers. Then his eyes strayed to the window and to the million stars twinkling in the great Montana sky. His eyes settling on one, he made his wish.

That his favorite star and fairy princess would have her happy ending.

9

"AND DON'T RUN OFF without this Chanel cream." Momentarily stopping her agitated pacing, Ellen thrust the black-and-gold jar into Jackson's hand. "With those rough calluses of yours, Mrs. Simpson, you'll need it. And you *promise* you'll call me and Wyatt the second you get to Denver? I mean, the *second*. You won't forget?"

As Jackson clutched the red pocketbook and mustered the infernal falsetto for what he prayed was the last time, his hungry eyes drifted over Ellen's adorable, long-sleeved pink minidress, which she was wearing with black tights and her combat boots. "Yes, m'dear."

"And here..." Ellen swiftly leaned and tugged the hem of Jackson's navy-and-white striped jumper. "That darn hem's crooked again. You can't get on a plane like that. And you're all packed? You have the numbers I gave you—for my agent, manager and Abel? Now, promise me you won't forget the numbers because those people always know where to reach me. Wyatt will, too, of course."

Eyeing the door, Jackson tried to convince himself that it was the only thing left between him, Ellen and a fairy-tale happy ending. But none of this was going exactly as planned. Why did one little white lie never seem to be enough? As soon as he'd told one, he'd had to tell countless others to cover his tracks. "Well, I must run along, m'dear. As I said, I called a cab and I'll miss that puddle jumper in Silver Spoon.''

''I still don't understand why you won't let me and Wyatt drive you. Are you sure you want a cab?''

''Oh, yes.''

''Well, I just hope your sister's all right. And you're *positive* that hospital in Denver will run the rest of the tests this afternoon?'' Ellen wrung her hands worriedly. ''I just can't believe there's nowhere for her to go if she's released from the hospital today. If she hadn't lost her apartment while trying to pay all those medical bills, at least there'd be a phone number for Wyatt and I to call.''

''There's no need to worry.'' Jackson couldn't stress that fact enough. ''*Really* no need, Ellen.''

But Ellen started pacing again, her lips compressed in fury, high color rising on her cheeks. ''I tell you, Mrs. Simpson,'' she fumed, ''we need to demand serious medical reform in this country. A nice woman such as your sister can't be penalized for getting sick. I mean, here she is, trying to make an honest living wage as a housekeeper—just like you, and now she's lost her apartment because she's been trying to do the right thing and pay her medical bills.''

Ellen halted in midpace, snatched a black leather backpack, whipped out a checkbook and started writing a check. ''Now, I want you to rent a nice apartment for your sister. The least we can do is make her comfortable. And if worse comes to worst—I mean, if she needs an operation or anything, which I'm sure she won't—don't forget I can always do a benefit concert.''

Jackson gasped. ''No! No benefit concert! No more money!''

Ellen shot him a stern look. ''There's pride, Mrs. Simpson,'' she declared, ''and there's *false* pride. Now, the most important thing is to ensure that your sister has a home. Don't forget, we're all in this together, so call and update me and Wyatt immediately.'' Ellen came forward, folding the check, but not before Jackson noted the amount had enough zeros to seriously intensify his guilt.

"I refuse to take that check—"

"There can be no price tag on friendship," Ellen reminded him firmly, deftly unclasping the red pocketbook. As she slipped the check inside, Jackson's heart beat double time. The fool purse was a mess— stuffed with lipsticks, crumpled tissues, truck keys, and a folded-up article on rising beef prices, which he'd been reading. He was horrified when he found himself wondering how men, himself included, ever functioned without a handbag.

"Knowing you and Wyatt has helped me so much," Ellen continued. "For years I've carried around so much anger about my life—about my father's drinking and the loss of both my parents. But now I feel as if a burden's been lifted. I feel as if I'm light as a feather and walking on air. I feel—"

"Please," Jackson interrupted. "That's enough."

"No, it's not. Because of you and Wyatt, I feel like a brand-new person."

Lordy, it was exactly what Wyatt had said to Jackson the day before. Trouble was, everybody to whom Jackson was giving a new lease on life was probably going to wind up wanting him dead. He edged toward the door, guessing he could rip up the check she'd written. He didn't know what to do about the envelopes of cash—the Simpsons' pay—which were in a drawer at home.

Ellen's eyes were now shining with unshed tears. "I'm going to miss you so much."

"I'll miss you, too." Even though he wasn't really going anywhere, Jackson could barely stand saying goodbye. Suddenly, illogically, he felt as if he was never going to see El again, and as her arms twined around his neck, terror seized his heart. She felt so good against him, so right. *Please, let me get away with this. Because I can't live another day without this woman.*

"I love you, Mrs. Simpson."

"I love you, too."

That much was the truth. Jackson reached behind him, his hand closing around the doorknob. *Two more seconds and you're through this door.* Then he'd come back with Wyatt and introduce himself as Jackson West. Sure, Ellen would be mad, but once he'd paid her back for this lousy shack, and seriously charmed her, she'd eventually forgive him. Maybe. Of course, if she ever found out he'd been impersonating Mrs. Simpson, he wouldn't have a chance. As far as Mrs. Simpson's supposed stay in Denver, he'd worry about that later.

Clearing his throat, he raised the pitch of his voice. "I'll be in touch." *And sooner than you think, El.*

"Goodbye, Mrs. Simpson."

"Goodbye, m'dear."

Sighing in relief, Jackson turned and opened the door. And then, as he stared through the screen, his whole body froze.

For a second, he thought he'd looked into a mirror.

A large woman with shoulder-length gray hair peered back at him through wire-rimmed glasses. She wore a blue turtleneck and a striped jumper similar to Jackson's, and she was now yanking open the screen door and preparing to swat him with a rolled-up newspaper.

"Mrs. Simpson?" Jackson gasped.

"Jackson West," Mrs. Simpson snarled, "what do you think you're doing, wearing my clothes?"

ELLEN DIDN'T ABSORB what was said—her mind just couldn't accept it. But she knew something was desperately, terribly wrong. For a second, the world seemed to stop revolving, and every last molecule of air seemed to be sucked out of the cabin.

Mrs. Simpson stared at Mrs. Simpson.

"Your sister," Ellen suddenly murmured, her first confused thought being that Mrs. Simpson's sick sister in Denver had been cured miraculously. But why would Mrs. Simpson's sister fly all the way from Denver to deliver the good news, when a phone call would suffice? And why would she look so furious about being well?

"You miserable cuss!" the lady on the porch suddenly shouted. Lunging across the threshold and into the cabin, she beat on Mrs. Simpson with the newspaper and swiped at her wig.

"Hold it right there!" Racing to Mrs. Simpson's defense, Ellen gripped the intruder's arm. But the woman wouldn't release Mrs. Simpson's wig. And because the wig was so securely pinned, poor Mrs. Simpson wound up doubled over, hopping forward and yelping as hairpins flew all over the floor.

Ellen tried to disengage the intruder's hold. Everything she'd learned in New York and L.A. came rushing back. She growled, "Back off, lady." And then things started happening so fast that Ellen couldn't even keep pace.

"Mother!" a man shouted, his footsteps pounding across the porch. "Mother, don't!"

"Wait, Wyatt!" yelled another woman.

"Thank heavens!" Ellen exclaimed. "Wyatt's here!"

But the man who burst through the door wasn't Wyatt. He had black hair, dark eyes and a mustache. He was the water boy from the football picture in Wyatt's room. "Wait a minute!" Ellen exclaimed. "What's going on here? You can't burst into my house this way! Who do you think you are?"

"Wyatt," said the black-haired man. "Wyatt Simpson."

"And I'm Darla West..." A jeans-clad cowgirl with honey hair and blue eyes tumbled breathlessly into the room and doubled over, gasping for breath. "I'm so pleased to meet you. We spoke on the phone a little over a month ago. I'm the one who set you up with Mrs. Simpson. I know you're going to hate me for it, and I don't blame you one bit. But before you get mad, I just want to take the opportunity to say I really love your records—"

"Quit hitting me."

The gruff masculine voice sounded behind Ellen. How had yet another *man* gotten in here? Ellen hadn't heard anyone come in the back door. She whirled around.

Ducking the blow of the rolled newspaper, Mrs. Simpson said, "Stop it!"

And she *was* a man.

Ellen's heart thudded hard. "Oh, no," she whispered.

She'd seen a lot of very strange things in New York and L.A., but nothing could have prepared her for this. Mrs. Simpson's gray wig was hanging by a bobby pin. And beneath the wig was a shock of thick honey hair—Wyatt's hair. The blue-framed eyeglasses and red pocketbook had been knocked to the floor, and the man's breasts were akimbo.

With a final blow of the newspaper, the woman— the real woman—snarled, "You deserve a lot worse, young man."

Ellen's eyes darted around wildly. Speaking to no one in particular, she said in a horrified whisper, "He's dressed up like his mother. He's wearing his mother's clothes. Tell me it's not true. Tell me I'm seeing things. Tell me…''

Ellen gulped. It took all the strength she had, but she forced herself to make eye contact with…*him*. Her pulse was ticking wildly in her throat. Her mouth was bone-dry. Before this moment, she'd thought herself the most liberal person in the world. A lifetime with her father had taught her to be tolerant and flexible.

But this was Wyatt. *Wyatt.* ''Whatever your… preferences,'' she managed to croak, ''I—I'll still try to…be your friend.''

He didn't say anything.

She said, ''Wyatt?''

''What?'' said the man with the black hair and mustache.

Suddenly, Ellen felt very confused.

''Like I said, I'm Darla,'' the honey-blonde rushed on in a strained cheerleader voice, ''and I couldn't be more pleased to meet you, Ellen. Why, I know how funny all this must look. But you're from the big city. So you must have seen some pretty weird things. Besides, there's a very reasonable explanation. Why, in a minute, I bet we'll all be laughing and joking about this silly little mix-up. Why, isn't it funny already? C'mon, what do you say? Why don't we all sit down—Mrs. Simpson, Wyatt, Jackson?''

Jackson? This time, Ellen heard it. But she couldn't respond. She was in overdrive. Seized by panic, she had an irregular heartbeat, an unnaturally heavy pressure burdening her chest.

''Reasonable explanation?'' she echoed.

For another full minute, the air got sucked out of the cabin again. Not a molecule moved.

And then everybody started chattering—and it sunk in fast.

When she finally spoke, Ellen couldn't believe how calm her voice was. Dead calm. Dangerously calm. "Now, let me get this straight. It started out as a bar bet. Then Jackson West dressed up in Wyatt's mother's clothes, and I hired him as my housekeeper. All this time, Wyatt's been in the hospital and Mrs. Simpson's been living quietly in Silver Spoon, working as a waitress. This morning she saw a picture in the newspaper with her look-alike identified as my housekeeper, so she came back to town, to find Wyatt, and to find out who was pretending to be her. Is this correct?"

Jackson West's sigh of relief made Ellen feel more murderous than she ever had. "That's it, El," he said.

How dare he use that nickname? Raw fury rushed through her veins. Only vaguely aware that he was now starting to plead with her, she let her eyes flit slowly over him, over the honey-colored hair beneath the lopsided wig, over the cockeyed breasts. Finally she took in the eyeglasses and pocketbook that had been knocked to the floor.

"Everything just got out of hand," he was saying. "It all went too far...."

The only thing that had gone too far was Ellen's willingness to open herself up. She'd shared herself—her thoughts and body, all the sweetness that was buried deep inside her. Oh, she'd known unreliable, horrible men—beginning with her father, but this was cruel beyond belief. Her insides starting shaking, until her belly was like jelly and her knees started to buckle.

"Please, El, hear me out."

"So, you're Jackson West." Turning calmly, Ellen headed for the corner. Lifting the rifle, she spun on her heel and aimed it right between his eyes.

To his credit, he said, "Go ahead and shoot me. I deserve it."

Her growl was venomous. "Just get out."

He might be a man of few words, but he was sure talking fast now. "I want to say one thing first. I love you. It started out as a bet, but I got to know you. And being dressed in that dress—I mean, *this* dress—I got to know you the way I never have known another woman. As a person, as a friend, as a—"

"Get out of this lousy shack you sold me or I'll shoot."

Darla, Wyatt and Mrs. Simpson started begging her not to pull the trigger.

Raising his hands slightly at his sides, Jackson edged toward the door, never taking his eyes from the gun. The glasses he'd been wearing crunched loudly underfoot. "I know I'm not real good at talking about my feelings," he continued, "but I—I really do love you. I swear, I never wanted to hurt you." His voice suddenly snapped. "Oh, El, sugar, this is breaking my heart. I…I want us to get married."

That was rich. "Marry this!" she exploded.

And then she pulled the trigger.

Fire flashed from the barrel with a boom—and a kick that sent Ellen staggering back. Wood ripped from the doorway as a bullet lodged.

"I guess that's a no," Jackson murmured.

"You got it, cowboy." Regaining her footing, Ellen stormed forward, her blazing dark eyes boring into Jackson's, while Darla, Wyatt and Mrs. Simpson hit the deck. "I said move!"

Jackson moved—and fast. His face was chalk white now, his blue eyes wide. He knew her well enough to be acquainted with her temper. He backed through the door, loudly cursing the day he'd taught her how to aim and fire. Ellen ran right after him, backing him off the porch and then all the way down the hill. Sweat from fury beaded on her upper lip.

As she forced him onto the paved road, he said, "I can't live without you."

"One more word and you might not live at all."

"But please…"

No, Ellen suddenly decided. He wasn't moving nearly fast enough. So, aiming to the left, she pulled the trigger again. Then again. Pain exploded in her shoulder from the kicks.

Uttering a string of oaths and ignoring the bullets whizzing past, Jackson drawled, "C'mon, I know I'm just a dumb cowboy, sugar. I've done a lot wrong in my life. Drinking, late nights, gambling—you name it. But because of you, I've given up every one of those vices. I'm not the man I was when I first met you. When we met—"

"Keep talking and who you'll meet is your Maker."

"Just listen—"

"I don't want to hear another word!"

Without the gun, she knew she wouldn't have stood a chance. He'd have gathered her in his arms, pressed kisses in her hair and sweet-talked himself into her good graces. Now she just wished he'd quit pleading. It was tearing her apart inside. Making her want to stop and talk it out. And yet it was so much easier to run again. Easier to pretend she was Annie Oakley in a Wild West movie.

"I felt so sorry for you, because of all your tragic losses," she snarled.

"I *have* had tragic losses."

She readjusted her grip on the rifle. "Well, you're about to have another."

His ragged, broken voice made her heart ache. "Please put down the rifle. Just listen. You've changed me, El. Changed my life. Everything's different now."

"Maybe for you."

"For you, too. For both of us."

"Not anymore. I can't believe what you did. I slept with you. I'd never slept with *anybody*. I trusted you. I told you all about my life." She'd lain naked in his arms. Bathed with him. Explored him intimately, with her hands and lips and tongue. There was no part of her—body or soul—that this man hadn't touched. She'd been a fool. But she'd opened up, surrendered, given herself...

Oh, she really wanted to kill him.

"Please, El. Think of what we stand to lose."

"What?" she said. "Your life?"

"No. *Our* life. The life we can share."

She glanced around. They were far down the road now, past the end of Little Miracle Lane, far past the Simpsons' cabin. "I'll think about that when I'm back in New York. Or L.A. When I've blown out of this stupid backwoods town of yours."

He stopped walking, seeming to run out of words.

And suddenly Ellen's heart wrenched—it squeezed and pulled, hurting like nothing she'd ever felt before. Because Jackson West's narrow, dreamy blue eyes looked suspiciously bright. And she knew this was one cowboy who had never cried.

His voice shook. "I love you," he said again.

And then, with the warm breeze ruffling that ridiculous dress, he turned and started walking down the road.

"I'M FINE," Jackson growled. Just when he'd thought things couldn't get any worse, minister Martin had appeared.

"Are you sure I can't offer you a lift?" The minister was hunched over the steering wheel of his blue compact car, driving at a snail's pace, peering between the windshield and his rolled-down window. "Please, Jean, talk to me. Are you all right? I don't know if I should say this, but your wig looks a little crooked. Are you crying? It looks like you're crying."

Hell no, Jackson wasn't crying. Maybe his nose stung a little. But he hadn't even cried when his daddy died. Blinking away the sting in his eyes that he told himself was from dust, he emitted a soft curse. Only one thing was certain: Ellen could never despise him as much as he despised himself.

"Can't you tell me what's happened, Jean? I know it was presumptuous of me, after the service on Sunday, to ask you on a date, but let's put that behind us now. At this moment, I am merely a man of God. And I am here to help in any way I can."

"Really," Jackson managed through clenched teeth, "I'm fine."

"Jean. Please, I'm begging you. As the leader of your parish…"

Jackson simply couldn't take it anymore.

Circling minister Martin's car, Jackson got in and slammed the door. He didn't even bother with the falsetto. "Take me to the Wests' ranch."

Minister Martin worriedly clutched the wheel. "The Wests?"

Jackson nodded.

"Whatever you need, Jean."

And then the man simply started to drive. Maybe it was just as well Jackson had gotten into the car he had stopped. Ellen had run Jackson all the way down the road, way past the trees under which he'd hidden his truck. From here, it would take him an hour to get home if he walked.

But what was he going to do? Ellen's whole demeanor had changed in a heartbeat. Oh, even as she'd squeezed the trigger of the rifle, her hands were shaking, and pure hurt was in those big brown eyes—not to mention tears. But she didn't exactly look forgiving.

Not that he was going to lose her. Hell, no. Jackson wouldn't give up that easily. He'd do anything—absolutely anything—to win her back. And the first thing he had to do was get out of this ridiculous jumper.

Fortunately, Mr. Martin drove fast, at least for a preacher. In fact, he was so worried about Jean, he was driving the compact car as if it were an EMS vehicle. Or Cinderella's coach racing home before it turned into a pumpkin again.

"Now, Jean," minister Martin said as he screeched to a halt in front of the ranch, "you'll call to talk if you need to?"

Jackson took in the widower's expression, the brown eyes so touched with concern, the crinkled forehead and worried frown. His heart softened. Oh, why not make the poor guy's day? It was the Christian thing to do. Besides, he, for one, knew what it was like to be spurned by a woman. Mustering his most convincing soprano, Jackson fluttered his eyelids and softly crooned, "Why, I simply don't know what I would have done without you today, Mr. Martin."

The minister positively beamed. "You're so welcome, Jean."

Jackson got out and shut the door. As soon as the minister's compact disappeared, he ripped off the wig. Then somehow, he endured the next few minutes, as he headed past the corral, ignoring the bugging eyes of the cowhands, their cat calls and wolf whistles. Inside, his brother Austin stopped in the front hallway and merely gaped. And then Jackson's mother appeared, clutching at her blouse collar saying, in a slow, uncertain voice, "Well, boys will be boys."

Upstairs, Jackson put his behind where it belonged—back into a pair of snug-fitting denim pants. Then borrowing the keys to Austin's ancient truck, he headed back out the door.

"No problem," Jackson muttered to himself. He'd get Ellen back. This was no big deal. Just a small glitch in his plans. Besides, he'd known she'd be mad, hadn't he? Yeah, this was nothing. In fact, hadn't he been expecting this?

"She'll forgive me," he whispered, rolling down his window and gunning the motor of the old pickup.

Pausing at the gate to the ranch, Jackson looked both ways.

Then the worst imaginable thing happened.

A bright white Land Rover roared past.

And a second later, Ellen Smith, a.k.a. Purity, had left Miracle Mountain, Montana, leaving Jackson West choking on her dust.

IN THE WEEKS that followed, there were a lot of changes around Miracle Mountain.

Without ceremony—or so much as a ribald snicker from the regular cowboys—Dusty quietly removed Purity's black leather, silver-studded corset from the moose above the bar, and neatly packed it away in the safe in the back office.

The real Mrs. Simpson, who had long been sober and living serenely in Silver Spoon, was reunited with her son and moved back home, and everybody in Bernadette's general store kindly remarked on the positive changes in Mrs. Simpson's appearance, attributing them to one of Darla's makeovers. With her good reputation already restored, she took up the mantle of one of the most respectable churchwomen in town. It was widely rumored that she immediately began dating the sweet lonely widower, minister Martin.

Jackson was another story.

With cowboy stoicism, he fulfilled his duties at the ranch by day. Nights, he came down to Dusty's and nursed the same cola until midnight, tapping the toe of his boot gently to the sad country-western tunes that poured from the jukebox. But he looked sadder than all those songs combined. People said he just wasn't the same man anymore, that his craggy cowboy face was starting to look downright haggard, and that a certain twinkle had left his once-bright, soft blue eyes.

Jackson just said that this was what could happen to a man, if he got in touch with his female, sensitive side.

Night after night, while he nursed his sodas, Jackson would imagine Ellen's return. He'd be trotting around the corral on his favorite cutting horse when that gleaming white Land Rover would barrel down the ranch driveway.

Or he'd be in the kitchen, yawning and putting on the morning coffee—and there she'd be, standing at the back door, with her brown eyes misty and forgiving, and her smile as bright as all the sunshine in the world.

Their reunion was always joyous. They'd both be talking at once. With him admitting he was a no-good scoundrel, and saying that he should have known better and never made that bet with Logan Hatcher. And with her saying her past had made her prickly, and that it was hard for her to forgive him, but that she knew what a lonesome cowboy he really was, and that she loved him more than life.

And then they'd smile and cry and hug each other and—

"C'mon, Jackson," Dusty said. "Why don't you let me get you a fresh cola?"

"Don't reckon I need it."

Dusty sighed. "You've got to snap out of this."

There was a long silence. And then Jackson sagely said, "Dusty, you can't snap out of love."

It was all he ever said.

Dusty rested his elbows on the bar. "Thing is, *we*

love you, Jackson. And everybody is worried sick. It's like you're gonna waste away or something. Where's our old Jackson, huh?''

The old Jackson was as long gone as Ellen. And now he sighed, seeing the questions behind Dusty's eyes. No one really knew exactly what had happened—they thought Purity had dated Wyatt, who had lost her to Jackson, who had lost her for good. No one knew the whole truth, or the connection between Jackson's being spotted at the ranch one day in a dress and his relationship with Ellen Smith. That they'd never know the whole story was the only saving grace, Jackson thought.

Reaching out, he clamped a manly hand on Dusty's shoulder and squeezed. "Thanks for the concern."

Dusty sighed again. "Just don't give up on her."

Jackson nodded. But it was no use. Weeks ago, he'd been so fired up and sure he could get Ellen back. When the Land Rover left him in the dust, he'd given chase, driving his heart out, pushing Austin's old good-for-nothing truck to its limits, until it sputtered to a halt a mile outside of Silver Spoon.

After that, Jackson called the numbers Ellen had given him—for her agent, her manager and Abel. But they'd been given strict orders not to let him through. A wall of people suddenly appeared, standing between him and Ellen, but Jackson still hadn't given up.

He'd bought a ticket and flown to L.A. And in a fancy hotel he'd kicked right through the door of the room where Ellen was supposed to be staying. Inside, he'd found a scared lady in a caftan, who cradled her bow-decorated poodle and called hotel security.

That was when Ellen had taken out a restraining order against Jackson. Now he had no idea where she'd gone. He had no untried phone numbers, no addresses. Nothing. And Darla had read that El had signed a new contract with the Trash Cans. That meant her plans involved making records and touring, not Jackson West and Montana.

It was all Jackson could do to get through a day. Most of the time, he wished he'd never met her. Because she'd opened up his heart and made him feel a thousand things that were all akin to pain and suffering.

"I bet you're still mooning after Ellen Smith?"

The voice came from behind him. His heart hitched, but he didn't bother to turn around. Hell, for a second there, it had sounded like Ellen. But he knew better. A thousand times he'd heard that voice. Or seen a glimpse of her on the street. He'd turn around or take off running—only to find a stranger. "No bets," he said, sipping at his soda. "I'm no longer a gambling man."

The voice was softer now. Tender. Unmistakably hers. "Jackson."

He swallowed hard. Believing—but knowing he was a fool to believe. Swinging around on the stool, he was sure it was just one of his countless fantasies. "Ellen?"

"Yeah."

His heart lurched. Instinctively he rose to his feet, his voice a mere whisper. It was really her. She didn't move, just watched him. And his eyes drifted over her, over her brown eyes and full lips and fuzzy wool dress. He'd never been so glad to see a pair of pink combat boots in his life. He wanted to put his arms around her and hold her tight, but her stance said her defenses were still up, that she didn't want to be touched.

With a finger, she more firmly pressed her granny glasses to the bridge of her nose. "Aren't you going to ask me why I'm back?"

She sounded so cool, so distant. He hoped against hope she'd returned because she wanted to make up. "Why?"

"Well…when I was packing, Wyatt and Darla told me what you did."

"What I did?" Jackson didn't have a clue.

"How you've helped Wyatt all these years. And how you put him in rehab because of what I said about enabling people. And Darla told me about all the private donations you've made to the church and the school and the hospital…."

Jackson winced. He'd been so sure nobody knew.

"And Wyatt said the only reason you wanted that land from Logan was because your father always wanted it, for a southern access road to the ranch."

Getting that land would have fulfilled Jackson's daddy's dream. But damn if he'd take it now. When Logan had tried to give him the deed to the land, he'd refused. His throat felt tight. "Underneath it all, I can be a good man, El. And I can be better, if you give me half a chance."

"I know you're a good man. I would have come back eventually because of that. But…well, I don't know how you're going to take this, but I came back because…"

His heart was pounding like the devil. Was something wrong? Was El in trouble? What could he do to help? "Because?"

"I'm pregnant."

Jackson could merely stare. "With a baby?"

Her lips curled in the faintest semblance of a smile. "Jackson, that's usually what it's, uh, with."

"Oh, Lordy." It was all he could say. Sitting down hard on the bar stool, he swallowed around the lump in his throat and rested his shaking hands on her waist, touching her as if she were made of glass. Then he stared into her eyes, stunned. This woman could sure knock the wind clear out of him.

She peered back, looking concerned. "Is your stomach turning turtle?"

"Definitely." Before he even knew what he was doing, he'd wrapped his arms around her waist and drawn her close, pressing his cheek against her belly. Then the words suddenly came. "We're having a baby? El, can you please forgive me? Maybe marry me someday?"

"I want to be with you, Jackson. But..." When he leaned back, her eyes were glistening with tears. "If only you'd trusted in our relationship enough to tell me the truth. If only things hadn't gone on so long. If only..."

"Sugar, my life's become a living hell of if-onlys."

Her eyes clouded. "You know all about me and my life. I can't easily trust and forgive."

"Just don't quit trying. I mean what I say, El. I want a life with you."

"We'll see."

Jackson had never felt so humble. "Can I kiss you?"

That fledgling smile tugged at her lips again. "I wish you would."

He cupped her face, his thumbs tenderly stroking her cheeks. He forgot the bar and all the cowboys looking on. There was only El. *His* El. The most beautiful woman in the world. The woman who was carrying his child. As he rose, drawing her against his chest, she seemed so delicate and fragile. His soft drawl was a solemn vow. "I swear I'll never hurt you again." And then he angled his head down to brush his mouth over hers.

Between his featherlight touches, she huskily said, "I want to be with you, Jackson. It's just going to take a while."

But nothing mattered now. Jackson's heart was bursting with joy and hope. This was all he'd prayed for—just this one chance to win her heart again. "For you," he whispered, as his warm mouth descended to savor the sweet taste of hers again, "there's all the time in the world."

Epilogue

FORTUNATELY, IT DIDN'T take all the time in the world for Ellen to forgive and marry Jackson. It took only until a crisp Montana evening, the week before Christmas. Miracle Mountain was in its full glory, the distant mountain peaks blanketed with snow, the lamps on the main street tied with red bows. In Bernadette's general store, Christmas carols played and the scents of cut pine and cinnamon wafted through the air.

Farther north, at the Bar Triple Cross, a giant wreath graced the gateway to the new southern road access—Ellen had happily accepted the land deed from Logan as an engagement present. Inside, the ranch smelled like heaven from Marilla's round-the-clock cooking, and next to the decorated tree, on the mantel, hung a new stocking Crystal had knitted, and on which was lovingly hand stitched the name, Ellen West.

That year, an "anonymous" contribution that everyone knew came from Jackson West paid for the new nativity scene at the Church of the Lamb. And spotlighted under the soft silver Montana moon, Mary, Joseph and the baby looked so solemn and peaceful that even the least sensitive cowboys felt a twinge in their hearts as they drove past in their pickup trucks.

It was inside the church, on that cold crisp December evening, that Jackson and Ellen solemnly exchanged their vows, with minister Martin presiding and the whole town of Miracle Mountain looking on.

"Have I told you you're beautiful?" Jackson murmured an hour later in the rec center, where the reception was held. Snuggling behind his bride, Jackson circled his arms around her waist, letting his hand drift over her white velvet gown, to her belly.

Ellen tilted her head, gazing up at him. "A million times."

He smiled. They'd posed for pictures and cut the cake, and he was glad to finally capture this moment alone with her. Gazing at her, he still felt as if he was living a dream. He sighed and pressed kisses into her hair, in which Darla had entwined baby's breath.

"And have I said I'm real excited about the baby?"

Color warmed her winter pale cheeks. "Oh, I think you might have mentioned that, too, Jackson. At least a gazillion times."

He grinned, nuzzling her neck. Every day, he waited to feel the child softly kicking against the palm he laid on her belly, and he'd imagine how El would look a few months hence.

Ellen sighed contentedly. "Well, you've got to admit, this is probably the strangest mix of people ever gathered in Miracle Mountain."

Jackson glanced up from her wondrously silken shoulder, and looking around the rec center, chuckled softly. Up front, on a stage, Abel Rage—dressed in the only black leather tuxedo Jackson had ever seen—was crooning an old Frank Sinatra number that didn't even vaguely resemble heavy metal music.

Jackson said, "His voice isn't half-bad."

"Don't tell him that, I'll be out of a job."

Jackson merely grinned. Abel Rage was definitely Jackson's most unlikely friend. For the life of him, Jackson didn't understand leather pants, tattoos or body piercing. No more, perhaps, than the kindhearted churchwomen fully understood the pink combat boots that protruded from beneath the robe of their newest choir member. Nevertheless, Ellen was in the choir, and Jackson and Abel were deeply united in their concern for Ellen. And with Ellen pregnant, Abel had been more than decent. He'd use her in the recording studio alone, and she'd no longer be traveling or playing in clubs. Ellen's agent was even talking about other jobs, maybe voice-overs for animated movies and kids' cartoons. For weeks now, Ellen had been flying between Montana, New York and L.A. And Jackson had realized that if you had a record company expense account and didn't mind flying, L.A. wasn't all that much farther away than Silver Spoon.

"Look," Ellen said throatily. "Minister Martin's dancing with Mrs. Simpson again."

"I think she's finally forgiven me," Jackson murmured. Fortunately, Mrs. Simpson had been no more inclined to talk about the past incidents than Jackson was.

Ellen's smile belied her words. "Even if I never will."

"Maybe," Jackson replied. "But you married me, El."

"In sickness and in health," she agreed pointedly.

He laughed. Everything seemed perfect. Even Darla and Wyatt were huddled together, near the cake table. Wyatt was still sober, and El was using her contacts in L.A. to try to establish Darla as a makeup artist. As for the churchwomen who were sure Jackson had stolen the girl from Wyatt, Jackson was quite content to let tongues wag, letting his bad reputation far outdistance his deeds, as had so often been the case.

Not so long ago, Ellen's agent had even forwarded an adorable thank-you note from little Sandra Sullivan, who said she was back in Wyoming, her leg completely healed. She'd enclosed a snapshot of herself on roller skates.

"Remember that night," El suddenly said softly, "when you said you wanted me to be with you during the holidays?"

"How could I ever forget?" Jackson's chest constricted. It was the night they'd made love for the first time.

Turning in Jackson's embrace, Ellen circled her arms around his neck. Tilting her head, she smiled up at him. "Well, I'm here. And it's Christmas."

Next year their baby would be there, too. Jackson's voice caught with emotion. "Merry Christmas, sugar."

"Merry Christmas, Jackson."

His ring was on her finger. His child grew in her belly. And yet Jackson still couldn't believe his good fortune. He shook his head in pure wonder. "El, every time I look at you, I thank my lucky stars." Lordy, that didn't even cover it. His chest ached, his stomach turned turtle and his heart was permanently lodged in his boots. He shook his head. "How a woman as perfect as you could have fallen for me, I swear, I'll never know."

Her deep throaty laugh was full of lust and life. "What girl could resist a cross-dressing cowboy?"

"So that was what did it, huh?"

"That," El said with a sigh, "and the fact you've got a lot of heart. And spirit." Her voice picked up tempo. "Oh, Jackson, there's so much good inside you. More than you'll ever know." Stretching, El tenderly touched her lips to his, in a way that left him aching for more. For all of her. "And," she added, "you've got the most important thing a woman could ever want and need in a man."

"Hmm?" Jackson murmured huskily, as his head angled down and his lips prepared to close over hers for the sweetest kiss in the world—one for all the holidays and love they were about to share. ''What's that?''

''A sensitive side.''

MEN at WORK

All work and no play? Not these men!

April 1998

KNIGHT SPARKS by Mary Lynn Baxter

Sexy lawman Rance Knight made a career of arresting the bad guys. Somehow, though, he thought policewoman Carly Mitchum was framed. Once they'd uncovered the truth, could Rance let Carly go...or would he make a citizen's arrest?

May 1998

HOODWINKED by Diana Palmer

CEO Jake Edwards donned coveralls and went undercover as a mechanic to find the saboteur in his company. Nothing— or no one—would distract him, not even beautiful secretary Maureen Harris. Jake had to catch the thief—*and* the woman who'd stolen his heart!

June 1998

DEFYING GRAVITY by Rachel Lee

Tim O'Shaughnessy and his business partner, Liz Pennington, had always been close—but never *this* close. As the danger of their assignment escalated, so did their passion. When the job was over, could they ever go back to business as usual?

MEN AT WORK™

Available at your favorite retail outlet!

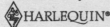 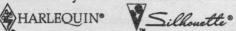

Look us up on-line at: http://www.romance.net   PMAW1

Not The Same Old Story!

Exciting, glamorous romance stories that take readers around the world.

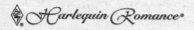
Sparkling, fresh and tender love stories that bring you pure romance.

Bold and adventurous— Temptation is strong women, bad boys, great sex!

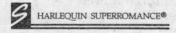
Provocative and realistic stories that celebrate life and love.

Contemporary fairy tales—where anything is possible and where dreams come true.

Heart-stopping, suspenseful adventures that combine the best of romance and mystery.

Humorous and romantic stories that capture the lighter side of love.

Catch more great

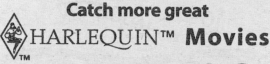

HARLEQUIN™ **Movies**

featured on **the movie channel** tmc

Premiering June 13th
Diamond Girl

based on the novel by bestselling author Diana Palmer

Don't miss next month's movie!
Premiering July 11th
Another Woman
starring Justine Bateman and Peter Outerbridge
based on the novel by Margot Dalton

If you are not currently a subscriber to The Movie Channel, simply call your local cable or satellite provider for more details. Call today, and don't miss out on the romance!

100% pure movies.
100% pure fun.

HARLEQUIN® *Makes any time special* ™

LOVE & LAUGHTER™

SEXY COWBOYS.
SASSY WOMEN. LOVE ON THE RANCH.

Don't miss these entertaining cowboy stories...

May 1998
#43 THERE GOES THE BRIDE
Renee Roszel

June 1998
#46 HOW THE WEST WAS WED
Jule McBride

July 1998
#48 COUNTERFEIT COWGIRL
Lois Greiman

August 1998
#50 GETTIN' LUCKY
Kimberly Raye

Stetsons, spurs and sparks make great romantic comedy.

Available wherever Harlequin books are sold.

LOOK FOR OUR FOUR FABULOUS MEN!

Each month some of today's bestselling authors bring
four new fabulous men to Harlequin American Romance.
Whether they're rebel ranchers, millionaire power brokers
or sexy single dads, they're all gallant princes—and
they're all ready to sweep you into lighthearted fantasies
and contemporary fairy tales where anything is possible
and where all your dreams come true!

You don't even have to make a wish...
Harlequin American Romance will grant your every desire!

Look for Harlequin American Romance
wherever Harlequin books are sold!

DEBBIE MACOMBER

invites you to the

HEART OF TEXAS

Join Debbie Macomber as she brings you the lives and loves of the folks in the ranching community of Promise, Texas.

If you loved Midnight Sons—don't miss Heart of Texas! A brand-new six-book series from Debbie Macomber.

Available in February 1998 at your favorite retail store.

Heart of Texas by Debbie Macomber

Lonesome Cowboy	February '98
Texas Two-Step	March '98
Caroline's Child	April '98
Dr. Texas	May '98
Nell's Cowboy	June '98
Lone Star Baby	July '98

HARLEQUIN®

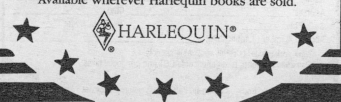

Don't miss these Harlequin favorites by some of our bestselling authors!

HT#25721	THE ONLY MAN IN WYOMING	$3.50 U.S.	☐
	by Kristine Rolofson	$3.99 CAN.	☐
HP#11869	WICKED CAPRICE	$3.50 U.S.	☐
	by Anne Mather	$3.99 CAN.	☐
HR#03438	ACCIDENTAL WIFE	$3.25 U.S.	☐
	by Day Leclaire	$3.75 CAN.	☐
HS#70737	STRANGERS WHEN WE MEET	$3.99 U.S.	☐
	by Rebecca Winters	$4.50 CAN.	☐
HI#22405	HERO FOR HIRE	$3.75 U.S.	☐
	by Laura Kenner	$4.25 CAN.	☐
HAR#16673	ONE HOT COWBOY	$3.75 U.S.	☐
	by Cathy Gillen Thacker	$4.25 CAN.	☐
HH#28952	JADE	$4.99 U.S.	☐
	by Ruth Langan	$5.50 CAN.	☐
LL#44005	STUCK WITH YOU	$3.50 U.S.	☐
	by Vicki Lewis Thompson	$3.99 CAN.	☐

(limited quantities available on certain titles)

AMOUNT	$ _____
POSTAGE & HANDLING	$ _____
($1.00 for one book, 50¢ for each additional)	
APPLICABLE TAXES*	$ _____
TOTAL PAYABLE	$ _____

(check or money order—please do not send cash)

To order, complete this form and send it, along with a check or money order for the total above, payable to Harlequin Books, to: **In the U.S.:** 3010 Walden Avenue, P.O. Box 9047, Buffalo, NY 14269-9047; **In Canada:** P.O. Box 613, Fort Erie, Ontario, L2A 5X3.

Name: _____

Address: _____ City: _____

State/Prov.: _____ Zip/Postal Code: _____

Account Number (if applicable): _____

*New York residents remit applicable sales taxes.
Canadian residents remit applicable GST and provincial taxes.

Look us up on-line at: http://www.romance.net

HBLAJ98